spring
mutsuki

Yuuki Haru

ISBN: 978-981-09-5696-7

To Mom

Table of Contents

Blue First Kiss 5

nostalgia fragrance 69

Infirmary Heart 81

In the Season of Falling Leaves 108

The Lagoon of Eyes 115

Commentary 164

Afterword 175

Blue First Kiss

I'm Mitsuki Aoi, just your average fifteen-year-old girl. I like sports, suck at math, and I'm in my first year at Ishigami High. Oh, and I'm a lesbian. But right now math is more important.

I sink into my chair with a groan. It's way past when anyone should still be in school but here I am, still sitting inside the student council's room long after today's meeting, butting my head against a brick wall of equations.

I can hear the sports clubs hard at practice on the grounds outside; they sound so far away it's like they're from a different world. Why do I have to be cooped up inside here when I could be out there? Well, homework, for one. At least it beats doing it at home.

I'm just about to restart my staring contest with the notebook in front of me, when the room door creaks open. Stepping into the room: Hiramoto Tsukasa, the girl of my dreams.

She's the picture of a cute beauty; petite, with curves in all the right places and brown eyes that sparkle in just the right way. But that's not all—even if, not that it would be possible in a million years, she were a beanstalk like me, she'd be just as beautiful. It's like, there's something inside her that shines, and you can just tell she's a good person.

"Aoi-chan!" Tsukasa-chan breaks into a smile, the moment she sees me. "You were still here?"

I smile back. "Hey, Tsukasa-chan."

"Homework?" She asks, walking up beside my desk.

I nod. "What about you? Did one of the teachers ask for help again?"

"Something like that. I was just about to go home, but I noticed the door wasn't locked, so..." She pauses, and looks over my shoulder at the mostly blank notebook in front of me. "Oh, math?"

"Yeah." I crack a sheepish grin. "It's due tomorrow, and I completely forgot about it until this afternoon."

"Oh. ...You know, I haven't finished mine either."

"Really?"

"Yup. So... if you'd like, maybe we could work on it together. It'll be more fun if we help each other out, after all, and it'll probably be easier too. Oh, but they're locking the gates soon, and the library's closed today. ...I know! Why don't you come over to my house?"

6

* * *

Setting her bag down, Tsukasa-chan gestures at the small table in the center of her room. "It's a little messy, but have a seat."

I do, and take a look around. The walls are a cheery canary yellow, but they're barely visible under the posters of constellations all over them. A huge bookshelf overflowing with photo books of stars dominates the far wall, and there's an actual telescope-tripod set folded up beside it.

"...Do you like astronomy, Tsukasa-chan?" I ask.

She gives me a shy smile, her cheeks turning pink. "...A little. M-More importantly, homework!"

"...Yeah." I chew on my lips, willing them not to turn up into a smile. This is the first time I've seen Tsukasa-chan so embarrassed, and it's way cuter than I ever could have imagined. It's not like I'm going to make fun of her or anything, geez...

My rapidly upswinging mood sinks like a rock, though, when I see her notebook; it's obvious she's miles ahead of me. She might have said we'd be helping each other out, but from the looks of things she'll be doing most of the helping. Talk about pathetic—if I'd known I was going to be mooching off Tsukasa-chan like this...

Catching the look on my face, Tsukasa-chan laughs. "You don't need to worry about it so much, Aoi-chan. Homework is more fun with company, right?"

"I guess so, but..."

"No buts. Now, why don't we get started?" She smiles at me, and my heart skips a beat.

"Y-Yeah, I guess you're right."

Working together, we finish our homework in no time. By the time we do, though, I'm already seeing rows of numbers on the backs of my eyelids.

I heave a sigh of relief, and lean back. "It's finally over!"

Tsukasa-chan giggles. "You were yawning the whole time, Aoi-chan. ...Was doing homework with me that boring?"

"W-Wha—no way! Y-You know, math is all thinky and stuff, so..."

"I know," Tsukasa-chan laughs. "I'm sorry, I just felt like teasing you a little." She pauses, taking a look out the window. It's almost evening. "Oh... I'm sorry, Aoi-chan, keeping you so late. Your house is on the other side of town, right? It's nearly dinner, too."

It's my turn to laugh. "It's fine. I'm used to going home

late, and my parents won't be back until midnight anyway. I'll just grab something from the convenience store."

"Then... how about having dinner here? If you don't mind, of course, but..."

'I'd love to!'—is what I'd like to say, but... "I couldn't, really. Not after you helped with my homework already."

"B-But... Oh, right! A-At least have a snack before you go!"

Urk. Tsukasa-chan's eyes shine, pleading with me. I know I shouldn't, but... "Well, if it's really okay..."

Tsukasa-chan sets a plate of cookies and glasses of milk to go with on the table, giving me a shy smile. "They're not much, really, but..."

No, they are—I've never seen cookies like these. They must be from some fancy bakery somewhere, they look so good. Wait, unless... "Tsukasa-chan, don't tell me, you made these yourself?"

Tsukasa-chan blushes, and nods.

The cookies look absolutely gorgeous; when I try one, I realize they taste even better. I'm having seconds before I know it. "Tsukasa-chan, these are amazing!"

"You're exaggerating, Aoi-chan."

"No, they are! They're really, amazingly—ack!" A chunk of cookie catches in my throat, and I start to cough.

"A-Aoi-chan!?"

I have to hit myself on the back, hard, and cough a few more times, before I can breathe properly again. That was a close one—I could have sworn I saw this bright light, and...

"Are you okay?" Looking up into my eyes, her expression radiating worry, Tsukasa-chan takes my hand in hers. My heart thumps, and honestly speaking I'm not very okay at all. I force myself to give her a smile, though, and nod.

She sighs in relief, then her expression turns stern. "Geez, Aoi-chan. The cookies aren't going to run away, so slow down."

"S-Sorry." I can feel my cheeks flush, and I want to curl up in a hole somewhere.

Tsukasa-chan just giggles. "I'm glad you liked them."

As we finish off the cookies, Tsukasa-chan turns to me with a suddenly serious expression. "You know, Aoi-chan... The truth is, there was something I wanted to tell you. That's why... that's the real reason I invited you over."

"Tsukasa...chan?" I freeze mid-sip, my glass of milk still

halfway to my lips.

...What? What did Tsukasa-chan just say, looking at me with those huge eyes of hers I wish I could swim in? No, I need to calm down—I'm definitely misunderstanding something.

"R-Really?" I stutter out. "So, uh, is it something to do with the student council? Oh, I got it—they're finally kicking me out, right? Geez, they could have told me directly, instead of..."

"Aoi-chan." Tsukasa-chan puts her hands on mine. "Please, let me finish." My brain grinds to a halt, and all I can do is nod.

Tsukasa-chan clasps her hands to her chest, and takes a deep breath. "I-I know it's weird, when we're both girls, but... Aoi-chan, for the longest time now, I've been in love with you. Will you go out with me?"

* * *

As I walk down the familiar road to school, my brain plays what happened yesterday in Tsukasa-chan's room on endless repeat. I have to pinch my cheeks every time it does; for the first time in my life, I think I understand what it feels like to be so happy it's like you're dreaming. After all, as of yesterday evening, Tsukasa-chan and I are officially going out!

My heart is so full it's bursting, and the world around me just seems to... shine. I feel like skipping the rest of the way to school, and I'm just about to when I see someone familar walking ahead of me—Yagami Seiko, my best friend. We've known each other since we were both in diapers, and she's like a sister to me.

"Seiko!" I call out, and run to catch up with her. "Good morning."

"...Aoi." Seiko squints at me, her eye bags as impressive as ever. "Mornin'."

"As gloomy as usual, huh."

"You're just too cheerful, grinnin' like that this early in the mornin'. What, somethin' nice happen?"

"Oh? Interested?"

"Not really," she sighs. "You're gonna tell me all about it anyway, right?"

Lunchtime. I walk as fast as I can through the rapidly filling school hallways, Seiko in tow.

"Well?" She asks, as she hurries to keep pace with me.

"Well what? You'll get wrinkles if you frown like that, Seiko."

"Oh, really? Thanks, Aoi—now if you've got time to worry about my complexion, mind tellin' me where we're goin'?"

I sniff, and turn my nose up. "I told you this morning, didn't I?"

"Aoi, don't tell me you're still poutin' about that—I said I was sorry for laughin', right?"

"Yeah, well..." We come to a stop in front of Tsukasa-chan's class, and I turn to Seiko with a grin. "Let's see if you'll believe me—"

The classroom door slides open, interrupting me. And, on the other side, Tsukasa-chan's look of surprise soon turns into a smile.

"Aoi-chan! I was just about to go get you!"

* * *

Tsukasa-chan, Seiko and I make our way to my number-one lunch spot, at the back of the school courtyard. The noon sun is high in the sky, but between the first winter winds and all the shade around us, its heat mellows to a pleasant warmth perfect for having lunch outside. The three of us find seats on the old stone benches lying around the courtyard, and we start laying out our lunches. Well, two of us do, anyway. I have one from the convenience store but Seiko is, rarely enough, empty handed. As for Tsukasa-chan, though...

"Wow!" I can't help but stare, as she undoes the cloth wrapping around her two-tiered lunch-box. It's a regular five-star feast, and if I wasn't used to seeing her normal lunches I'd swear it was from a restaurant. Of course, it's all homemade.

Tsukasa-chan blushes. "I-It's nothing special, really. I just woke up a little early today, so I thought I'd practice cooking something a little more complicated, that's all."

"There you go again, Tsukasa-chan. It looks fantastic! Right, Seiko?" I nudge Seiko in the ribs, and she grunts.

"...Hm? Oh, Hiramoto. Yeah, I guess." Looking about as uninterested as she could get still awake, she just yawns.

"Still half-asleep?" I sigh. "That's what you get for staying up all night. I bet you skipped breakfast again, too."

"Sure, you got me. ...Now, since that's how it is, you don't mind sharin', right?" Her yawn turns into a grin, then, in the blink of an eye, she strikes! Snatching a meatball out of my lunch-box—with her bare hands, too—Seiko swallows it in a single gulp, and burps. "Thanks for the treat, Aoi."

"Wha—Seiko!? I was looking forward to that!"

I'm about to give her a piece of my mind, when Tsukasa-chan interrupts me with a laugh. "You get along with Yagami-san so well, Aoi-chan."

A blush spreads across my cheeks, and I swallow the scolding on the tip of my tongue. "R-Really?" God, I must look dumb, fooling around with Seiko like this.

Tsukasa-chan shakes her head. "There's no need to be embarrassed. It's a good thing, isn't it? ...I'm a little jealous, even."

"Jealous?"

"Of course. The two of you look so close, it's like you're... sisters. I don't have anyone like that, so..."

"W-Well, you know..." My blush deepens; it's a little embarrassing, being told that right to my face. "...Seiko and I are best friends, after all."

"Best friends, huh."

"Tsukasa-chan? Did you say something?"

"I-It's nothing! Oh, right—I was just thinking, how about we exchange side-dishes, Aoi-chan? I'd love to try some of yours."

"Really? But..." Tsukasa-chan gazes into my eyes, hers shining, and my tongue forgets what I was about to say. "...But if you're fine with them, I'd love to."

"I'm glad. ...Oh, Yagami-san, if you'd like, I could share some with you too. You must be hungry, right?"

"...Appreciate it, but I'm fine." Seiko yawns again, and rolls over on her stone bench.

"Oh." Tsukasa-chan's face falls.

I shoot Seiko a glare. "Don't mind her, Tsukasa-chan. Come on, let's dig in."

By the time we finish eating, lunch is about to end. Tsukasa-chan had day-duty for her class so she went back first, and it's just Seiko and me now. ...Speaking of Seiko, for someone who didn't touch a bit of Tsukasa-chan's gorgeous cooking, she sure didn't hold back when it came to my already pathetic lunch, the glutton.

Lounging on her bench like a cat in the sun, Seiko gives me a look. "So you finally did it, huh? Aoi."

16

"What do you mean, 'finally'?" I scowl, but she just waves me off.

"I know, I know. I'm just teasin' you, that's all. I'm happy for you. Really. ...I mean, what kind of friend would I be if I wasn't?" She breaks into a grin, bits of lunch still stuck in her teeth.

"...Thanks." Make me blush, why don't you. I look away, so she can't tell how red my cheeks are getting, and offer her the spare toothpick from my lunch. "Here, your teeth. I can't let my best friend show a smile like that on campus, right?"

"I don't want to hear that from you, Aoi." Seiko laughs, and plucks a grain of rice from my face—and then she just pops it in her mouth!

"Wha—Seiko!?"

"Better be careful, Aoi—can't have you showin' a face like that on campus, after all."

"...Geez."

* * *

17

It's the end of homeroom, and I heft my bag and get ready to leave with Seiko, when I run into an angel in the hallway.

"Aoi-chan!" Tsukasa-chan calls out, and makes her way through the crowd of students towards us. She gives me a shy smile. "Homeroom ended early today, so I thought I'd come meet you. And, you know, I don't have anything on after school today, so... maybe we could walk home together?" She pauses, taking a look at Seiko. "...Ah, of course, you too, Yagami-san."

"Um..." I don't know what to say. I'm happy—no, overjoyed, even—that Tsukasa-chan wants to walk home together at all, but if we're going to be walking home, just the two of us would be nice... I give Seiko a glance, and she answers with a roll of her eyes.

"Don't worry about me, Hiramoto, I've got somethin' on today. See you, Aoi." Seiko gives me a wave, then she walks off.

Tsukasa-chan and I see her off, then Tsukasa-chan turns to me. "Aoi-chan. Why don't we get going too?"

"Yeah."

As we're walking home in nervous silence—mostly on my

part—Tsukasa-chan suddenly speaks up. "...Aoi-chan, was I interrupting something?"

"Just now?" I laugh. "Don't worry about it, Tsukasa-chan. Seiko and I didn't have any plans anyway."

"Oh. ...I thought so earlier too, but you call Yagami-san by her first name all the time, don't you?"

"Well, yeah. We've known each other since we were kids—anything else would be weird, right?"

"You're childhood friends?"

"Pretty much. It's a little like you said, I guess. Me and her are sisters by now."

"...You really do get along well, after all."

We walk in silence, for the next half-block, before Tsukasa-chan speaks up again. "A-Aoi-chan, I was thinking... this Sunday, if you're free, maybe... we could have a date?"

My heart doesn't just skip a beat, it stops completely; I feel like pinching my cheeks, even, to make sure I'm not dreaming. "O-Of course! I'd love to!"

"Really? I'm so glad!" Tsukasa-chan's eyes shine, pulling me in, and I happily drown in them. They spark something

19

inside of me, too, pushing me on; I can't let Tsukasa-chan take the lead all the time!

"T-Tsukasa-chan. It's getting a little cold, isn't it? And, look, since we're already walking together like this... do you want to hold hands?"

"...Yes. I'd love to." She smiles, and offers me her hand. I gulp, and take it. Even though we were touching just a moment ago, when my fingers brush against hers warm electricity courses through me, and I shiver. Our fingers intertwine—hers first, then mine following her lead.

I realize I'm staring at our hands, and shift my gaze back to Tsukasa-chan's face. It's at the same time she does, to mine, and our eyes meet. I freeze, fire erupting from my cheeks; she just giggles, and squeezes my fingers in hers. "Aoi-chan, your hands are warm."

"R-Really?"

"Yup, they are. Warm, and soft, and kind."

"...Then they don't suit me."

"They couldn't any better, Aoi-chan. You're the warmest person I know."

I laugh. "You're just flattering me."

"I'm not." Tsukasa-chan gives my fingers another squeeze.

"I mean, that's one of the things I love about you, after all."

My heart thumps in my chest, a regular marching band drum. It's so loud I can't believe Tsukasa-chan doesn't hear it.

...She's definitely flattering me now. How could I possibly be warmer than she is? It feels like I could just melt, standing by her side like this.

We start walking again, my hand in hers, and my heart pounding the whole time. I'm grinning like an idiot. God, this all feels like a dream, like my alarm is going to ring and catapult me back into boring gray reality any minute now. But, dream or not, I just wish we could stay like this forever.

In no time at all, though, we reach where we have to part ways. It's the bridge between Lower Ishigami, where my house is, and the Ishigami district proper, where Tsukasa-chan lives.

"It looks like this is it for today, Aoi-chan."

I nod. Neither of us let go of our hands. But, we took our time walking here, and it's getting dark. Never mind me, basically living on my own, Tsukasa-chan has dinner with her parents. No matter how much I want to, I can't keep her here. "...Let's enjoy this Sunday, okay?"

"I'm looking forward to it, Aoi-chan." Tsukasa-chan gives me a small smile. It's bewitching, in the orange-madder light of the setting sun.

* * *

The longest week of my life later, it's finally Sunday: the day of my date with Tsukasa-chan at last! I reach where we agreed to meet, the train station in the middle of town, fifteen minutes early. When I arrive, Tsukasa-chan's already there.

"Tsukasa-chan!" I call out to her—she turns around, and my mind goes blank. It's the first time I've seen her in casual clothes, and she looks absolutely gorgeous! She's wearing a cream blouse with a blue gingham pinafore and stockings, and an elegant straw sun-hat. I'm starting to feel under-dressed, in my plain old parka and jeans.

Tsukasa-chan greets me with a wave. "Aoi-chan! What are you doing here so early?"

"What about you? Did you wait long?"

"No, I just got here too. But, since we're both here already, why don't we get going?" She smiles, and offers me her hand. I smile back, and take it.

We head to the nearby Lower Ishigami Shopping District—or just Lower District for short. It's the place to shop around here, filled with all sorts of shops and boutiques; perfect for a date.

Tsukasa-chan's eyes shine, as she looks around. "Wow... so this is what the Lower District looks like. It's so big."

"Tsukasa-chan, you've never been here before?"

"I've heard the girls in class talk about it, but it's my first time."

"T-Then, why don't I show you around? This place is great, but there are so many shops here it's easy to get lost, and—"

Tsukasa-chan gasps, cutting me off. The next thing I know, she's off! To... a used bookstore? An old one too, with a yellowed signboard and boxes of books overflowing into the street.

"Look, Aoi-chan!" Tsukasa-chan holds up a book nearly as thick as all my textbooks combined. "It's a first edition collection of Hubble photographs! They went out of print years ago—I thought I'd never find one!" She holds the book in her hands like it's made of gold, her expression pure bliss.

"...You really like the stars, huh, Tsukasa-chan."

Making my way to her, I look over her shoulder as she lovingly runs her hands along the book's face. ...Not that I'm jealous or anything.

Tsukasa-chan turns to me, a beatific smile on her lips. "I love them! They're beautiful, of course, but... that feeling when you look up on a dark night and everything but you and the stars disappear, and you can have them all to yourself—I love it! Of course, that doesn't mean I don't like looking at them through a telescope, but..." Tsukasa-chan trails off, and she then gives me an embarrassed smile. "I-I'm sorry, Aoi-chan. I didn't mean to go on like that. It must have been boring, right? Listening to me ramble."

I smile. "Not even a bit. I mean, you looked like you were having so much fun."

"I-It's not weird? My liking the stars."

"Um..." To be honest, I don't really know. But, when I remember her smile just now... "I think it's wonderful. I mean, having something you can enjoy so much is a good thing, right? At least, I think so."

"Aoi-chan..."

Tsukasa-chan's cheeks flush pink, and my own follow her lead. "A-Anyway!" I say. "Since we're already here, why don't we take a look inside?"

Tsukasa-chan's gaze falls to the book in her hands, then back to me. "Are you sure? I mean, it's our first date, and..."

I laugh, a little sheepishly. "The truth is, after seeing you enjoy yourself like that, I started feeling like shopping for books too. Besides, we're having fun, so isn't it fine? First date or not."

"You're right, Aoi-chan." Tsukasa-chan beams, turning that gigawatt smile of hers on me. "Let's go in?"

When we leave the bookstore—with a 'new' used book for me and a whole bag of them for Tsukasa-chan—it's almost noon.

"Tsukasa-chan, where do you want to go next?"

"I'll leave it up to you, Aoi-chan."

"Then..." I stop to think. Clothes? I haven't actually gone into most of the boutiques here, but I know where are the main ones, at least. "How about..." I start to suggest one nearby, when a loud gurgle from my stomach cuts me off.

"Aoi-chan?" Tsukasa-chan asks, and a hot blush spreads across my cheeks. God, I wish there was a hole somewhere so I could crawl into it. But, she just smiles that smile of hers and... "You know, the truth is I was so excited I didn't eat any breakfast today. So, I was wondering... maybe we could get something to eat first?"

"O-Oh, really? Well, there's this great crepe stand around here, and..." Forgetting my embarrassment, I take Tsukasa-chan's hand and start walking.

* * *

Tsukasa-chan and I sit on a bench by the crepe stand, crepes in hand. I'm having vanilla caramel, and she's having strawberry.

Tsukasa-chan takes a nibble of her crepe, and her expression lights up. "Delicious!"

I laugh, in between bites of mine. "Yeah, this place is the best. I stop by every time I'm around here, they're so good."

"Do you come here often, then, Aoi-chan?"

"Yup. Mostly with Seiko, but I come by myself sometimes too. The air here just agrees with me, I guess."

"Oh, I see..."

"W-What about you, Tsukasa-chan? Do you have someplace like that?"

"M-Me? ...Well, I like going to the park by the old clock tower, I guess. There's never anyone else around, and you can see the stars there when it's clear out. It's so peaceful, I love it there."

"Wow. It sounds wonderful. M-Maybe... we could go there sometime. Together. A-And, you know, we could bring Seiko along, too! I bet she wouldn't appreciate it at all, that shut-in, but..."

Tsukasa-chan freezes mid-bite, then she takes a quick look at her watch. "...I'm sorry, Aoi-chan." She gives me a small smile, getting off the bench. "Actually, my parents are doing something at home this afternoon, so..."

"No way, really? Geez, I'm sorry—I should have asked, or..."

"No. No, it's my fault, Aoi-chan. Really. But..." She takes a sad look at the crepe in her hands, then she hands it to me. "We'll have a proper date next time, I promise, so..."

"Don't worry about it, Tsukasa-chan. More importantly, are you going to make it? I'll walk you back to the station."

"...It's okay. I'll be fine by myself. I can't make you walk all the way back, just for me. So... see you tomorrow, Aoi-chan."

* * *

Monday, just another school day; the one after my first date, that is. Okay, so it got cut a little short, but still. I'm so happy I'm humming as I walk to school.

Walking by my side, Seiko gives me an exasperated scowl. "...Aoi, would you stop grinnin' like that? It's creepy. Did you hit your head or somethin'?"

"Give me a break, Seiko, I'm just happy—there's nothing creepy about that."

She sighs. "Hiramoto again, huh? Should have known."

I just ignore her. Nothing's going to ruin my mood today.

When we reach the school gates, there's a huge commotion around them. Craning my neck, I try to peer into the mass of students milling about, but no luck. "I wonder what's going on?"

"Who knows. Let's just hurry and get inside, Aoi. It's freezin' out here."

"Yeah, I guess you're right."

We squeeze our way into the crowd; as we make our way through, though, I catch part of the crowd's murmuring.

28

"...collapsed?" "...girl ...which class..."

"...1-A."

Wait, that's Tsukasa-chan's class! N-No, calm down, me, there are like twenty girls in that class. What are the odds...

"Excuse me!" I raise my voice, and start shoving my way into the crowd. "Let me through, student council!" That's right! It might be mostly in name, but I'm a member of the student council. It's my responsibility to find out what's going on.

"Aoi!? Hey, Aoi!" Seiko's swallowed up in the crowd behind me, but I barely even notice, I'm so intent on finding out what's going on.

But, the moment I push my way through the crowd, my mind goes white. Lying there collapsed on the ground is—

"Tsukasa-chan!"

* * *

Stepping away from Tsukasa-chan's infirmary bed, the school nurse turns her attention to Seiko and I. "It isn't anything serious, just fatigue," she says.

29

"Thank you, Inokawa-sensei." We bow.

"This is my job, after all." She gives us a gentle smile. "I'll take care of her here—you two can go back to class now."

"...Oh." I bite my lip. "R-Right, of course." I know it's silly, but I can't help myself. I...

"...Well, I suppose you can't concentrate like this anyway."

"Inokawa-sensei?"

She shakes her head. "The truth is, I've got an errand I need to run, but I can't just leave Hiramoto-san here all alone. She'd be shocked, wouldn't she? If she suddenly woke up without anyone around. I don't suppose I could ask you to help look after her, Mitsuki-san?"

"Of course! ...Is it really okay?"

"If it's only until she wakes up, or I come back."

"Thank you, Inokawa-sensei!"

Inokawa-sensei just waves me off and leaves, sliding the door shut behind her. Next to me, Seiko lets out a huge yawn. "Well, that's that. Guess I'd better be headin' off myself."

"Yeah. Lend me your notes later?"

"Sure thing—long as you treat me to a meal sometime soon."

"Deal."

* * *

With Seiko gone, it's only me and Tsukasa-chan left. Crossing the room, I take a seat by her bedside. ...She looks so much better than when Seiko and I carried her in, but I still remember how pale she was, crumpled on the ground, and my chest starts to ache.

"Don't make me worry like that, Tsukasa-chan." I whisper, and reach out to brush her hair from her forehead. As I do, though...

"...Aoi-chan?" She stirs, opening her eyes.

"S-Sorry!" I pull my hand back. "...Did I wake you?"

Tsukasa-chan shakes her head, and gives me a sleepy smile. "I thought I heard your voice, so..." Getting up, she yawns, and takes a look around. "Where...?"

"You collapsed in front of the school gates, Tsukasa-chan."

"Oh." She sits, silent for a moment, then she gives me an embarrassed smile. "...I must have made a real scene, didn't I?"

I sigh. "You scared me, you know?"

"...I'm sorry, Aoi-chan."

"No, I'm just glad you're all right. Are you feeling any better? Inokawa-sensei said it was just fatigue, but..."

"I-It's nothing so serious, Aoi-chan, really."

"But you fainted, right? That's plenty serious."

"W-Well... The thing is..." Tsukasa blushes, and looks down at her lap. "I... I know why I fainted, I think, but... if I tell you, will you promise not to laugh?"

"Of course I won't, I promise."

"The truth is, last night, there was this... horror movie showing, and..." She trails off, her cheeks so red it looks like they're going to catch fire.

Tsukasa-chan looks so amazingly cute, all embarrassed like that, that before I can stop myself I'm shaking with laughter. "Geez, so that's what it was."

"A-Aoi-chan! You promised not to laugh, right?" Tsukasa-chan scowls. "You don't know how embarrassing it is, fainting because of... because of a stupid reason like that!"

"I didn't mean to, really. But, I was just so relieved it wasn't anything serious..."

"Aoi-chan... I'm sorry, worrying about me."

"W-Well, I mean, we're g-girlfri—we're going out, right?"

"...You're right. I'm... really sorry, Aoi-chan."

"Hm? About what?"

"...No, it's nothing. Thank you, Aoi-chan."

As Tsukasa-chan and I sit together in the infirmary, I hear the bell for first period ring outside. Oh, so it's that time already... wait. Wincing, I get off my chair. Darn, I was so engrossed with Tsukasa-chan I forgot all about my deal with Inokawa-sensei.

"Aoi-chan?" Tsukasa-chan looks at me, puzzled, and I shake my head.

"Inokawa-sensei said I could stay here with you, but only until you woke up. So... you know..."

"Oh." Tsukasa-chan's face falls. "You're going back to class?"

"...I promised, after all."

"B-But... oh, right!" Tsukasa-chan grabs me by the sleeve. "You know... the truth is I'm still... a little dizzy. So, maybe... you know, just in case...?"

I gulp. I shouldn't, I really shouldn't, not after Inokawa-sensei's already let me get away with this much. B-But, you know, I can't just leave Tsukasa-chan alone here. What if she fell, or something!

"Y-Yeah, I guess I should, then. Just in case."

* * *

As expected, I got a good scolding from Inokawa-sensei when she got back. Well, I guess it can't be helped. Tsukasa-chan really was still feeling a little woozy, too, so Inokawa-sensei ended up giving her permission to go home, and me to send her back just in case.

As Tsukasa-chan and I walk down the familiar road back home, holding hands, she suddenly speaks up. "...Are you really sure it's okay? Walking me back like this."

"Why?"

"I mean, you're missing classes all because of me."

I laugh. Tsukasa-chan is being way too considerate, as

34

usual. "Inokawa-sensei said it was, right? What if you collapsed again? Besides, I'll be back in school before lunch, so don't worry about it."

"...I guess you're right." Tsukasa-chan pauses, looking down at the ground and nibbling at her lips. Then... "Aoi-chan, I'm so sorry about yesterday. I really shouldn't have left so suddenly, especially after you made time for me too."

"It was something important, right? With your family. Then it can't be helped."

"That's... true, but..."

"No buts. ...I mean, I did want to spend more time together, but... maybe if you're free sometime soon... "

"W-Well... Aoi-chan, you don't have anything on tomorrow, right?"

"...I'm off day-duty, so yeah. Why?"

"I'm free too. So... let's have another one after school—a date."

* * *

Tuesday. The moment homeroom ends, I'm off to the school gates. When I arrive, though, Tsukasa-chan's already waiting. She greets me with a smile like the sun, and we start walking hand in hand down the road into town.

"Aoi-chan," Tsukasa-chan asks. "Is there anywhere in particular you want to go?"

"What about you?"

She puts a finger to her lips. "We ended up going where I wanted, last time, so... I'd really like it if we could go somewhere you want, today."

"Well..."

When we arrive at the Lower District, we make a beeline for its most famous store, the Ishigami Lumière Nova boutique. What's so special about it? It's only the most premium made-in-Japan clothes line in the world. The Ishigami branch is the first and only LN store outside New Tokyo, too! It's the crown jewel of the Lower District, and I've spent hours just dreaming about going inside—let alone with Tsukasa-chan. My imagination sends up a fireworks display of Tsukasa-chan in an LN outfit, and I swear I'm this close to a sudden nosebleed.

O-On second thought, maybe this is too much, for our second date. Yeah, that's right, we should take things slow, start somewhere a little less glitzy. I don't think my heart's going to make it, like this.

I'm just about to suggest we go somewhere else, when—

"You know, Aoi-chan... the truth is, I've always wanted to come here." Tsukasa-chan says. "But, I was always too nervous by myself. That's why I'm glad you're with me." She gives me a shy smile, and I freeze. There's no way I can suggest we turn around like this!

"R-Really?" I stammer out instead.

"Really. So, let's go in?"

The inside of the store is a mini fashion parade. From the staff to the other customers, even the displays look straight from some catwalk in Milan. I'm so out of place here it's not even funny.

Tsukasa-chan found something she liked right after we came in, so I'm waiting for her by the fitting rooms. As expected of LN, the staff didn't bat an eyelash at letting penniless students like us try on clothes; it was more like they were cheering us on, recommending one outfit after another with a smile. They're so friendly being nervous starts feeling silly.

B-Besides, it isn't like my heart's racing from being just a curtain away from Tsukasa-chan changing, or anything like that. Just because I'm worried I won't have the vocabulary to describe how beautiful she's obviously going to look doesn't mean—

The changing room curtain slides open, sending my train of thought off the rails. Standing on the other side, Tsukasa-chan fusses with the hem of her dress, her cheeks flushed pink. "H-How do I look?"

How does she look? Like an angel! Forget vocabulary, all I can do is stare.

"...Say something, Aoi-chan. Don't tell me, it looks weird?"

"No! Not in a million years! You look wonderful, Tsukasa-chan."

Her blush spreads to the tips of her ears. "Aoi-chan... E-Enough about me, you're not going to try anything on?"

I freeze. "Me?"

"That's why we came here, right?"

"But..."

"Aoi-chan." She looks at me, her eyes shining. I gulp.

The changing room is surprisingly roomy, and I didn't

have any trouble changing into the outfit Tsukasa-chan picked for me. The only problem is...

I sigh. I knew from the start LN might be a bridge too far for a beanstalk like me, but it's still depressing how terrible I look in such nice clothes. Time to change back into my uniform, the only skirt I'm ever going to be able to—

The changing room curtain slides open, to reveal Tsukasa-chan peeking in. "Oh. Aoi-chan, you've finished changing."

I freeze. "T-Tsukasa-chan!? What are you..."

"Shh." She puts a finger to her lips, coming inside, and sliding the curtain closed behind her. "You can't talk so loudly—what if someone heard?"

"B-But... what are you doing?"

"You were taking a while, so I wondered if you needed help with the dress..." She pauses. "Am I being a bother?"

"Not at all," I start to say, but my tongues tied into a know, and all that comes out of my mouth is mumbling.

Her face falls. "I am being a bother, aren't I."

"N-No, you're not!" I stammer out. "Y-You know, I was just surprised, that's all."

"But you won't even let me take a look at you."

"That's... I look ridiculous, don't I?"

Tsukasa-chan narrows her eyes at me—so this is how she looks when she's angry—and plants her hands on her hips. "Aoi-chan, why do you look down on yourself like that? You're beautiful." Her expression dares me to disagree.

I look away, blushing. "...You're just saying that."

"Believe me, Aoi-chan. That's how I really feel." Tsukasa-chan's scowl melts into a gentle smile, and she wraps her arms around me. "Don't say things like that about yourself, okay? You're beautiful, and cool, a real prince. That's why I fell in love with you, you know?"

"Tsukasa-chan..."

* * *

"...and then she invited me for another date this weekend!"

The first thing I do when I get home, after a microwaved meal and a bath, is to call Seiko and report today's date. But, instead of the celebration I was expecting, all I hear from her end is a sigh and the scratching of pencil on paper.

"That's great, Aoi, congratulations—not. What time do you think it is?"

"Come on, this is like afternoon for you. You could be a little happier for me, Seiko."

"Sorry, but I don't have any happiness to spare at twelve midnight."

Geez, talk about crabby. And she hasn't stopped scribbling for a second the whole time, too. ...Wait. "Seiko... don't tell me, you were busy?"

Another sigh, heavier. "Don't worry 'bout it, Aoi. I was goin' crazy just doin' all this drawin' anyway. ...Any more of your boastin' might be a little tough, though."

I crack a sheepish grin. "Yeah, got it. I'll let you get back to your work, then. ...Don't stay up too late, got it?"

"...Yeah. Night, Aoi. See you at school tomorrow."

"Night, Seiko."

I flip my phone shut and dive into bed. My brain has today's date on endless repeat, and every time I close my eyes I see Tsukasa-chan's face.

But, that's not all I remember.

"Beautiful and cool, huh?" That's the 'prince' Tsukasa-chan sees, someone completely different from me. But if that's the 'me' she likes...

"Tsukasa-chan..."

* * *

A week later, lunchtime. Tsukasa-chan's been swamped doing student council work for the end of term celebrations lately, and she's never in class. So, it's just me and Seiko, again. We're eating in the cafeteria instead of class, for a change at least.

Seiko takes a seat next to me, setting her tray down besides mine. Today's special, an oppressively red bowl of Mapo Tofu Surprise, takes pride of place, and it matches her expression perfectly.

"Why so down, Seiko?" I ask in between bites of my sandwich. "It's a beautiful day."

"To you, maybe." Prodding at her food, Seiko scowls at me. "Shouldn't you be leavin' me in peace and eatin' boxed lunches with Hiramoto?"

"Give me a break, even I'd get sick of eating convenience store food every day. ...Besides, Tsukasa-chan wasn't in her class."

"Really. Too bad, bein' stuck with just little old me."

I roll my eyes. "Geez, you know that's not how it is. You haven't answered my question, either. Work?"

"Yup. Got a bunch of promisin' drafts comin' back for revisions this week. ...More importantly, Aoi." Looking up from her food, Seiko points her Mapo-red spoon at the crowd of students waiting for seats. "Ain't that your very busy Hiramoto?"

"Oh, it is." I spot Tsukasa-chan immediately; she's wandering about and looking for a seat, tray of food in hand.

Seiko sighs. "Go help her out already. She's goin' to be stuck there until lunch ends, at this rate."

"Thank you, Aoi-chan." Walking by my side, Tsukasa-chan beams at me as I lead her back to our table. "It's my first time here, so..."

I grin back at her. "Don't worry about it. More importantly, are your duties with the council okay?"

"It was nothing big, really. ...I heard you came by, when I got back to class, so I thought I might run into you, and..." She trails off, just as we reach the table Seiko and I are sharing. "...So you were eating with Yagami-san."

"Hm?"

"N-No, it's nothing. I was thinking how nice it must be, to be such good friends."

"Really? I think it's pretty normal, though. We've eaten together a few times too, right?"

"Yes, but..." Tsukasa-chan shakes her head. "Why don't we sit down first?"

"Yeah, you're right—hey, Seiko, scoot your tray over a little."

"It's okay, you can have it, Aoi." Seiko pushes her tray away, then she gets up and gives Tsukasa-chan a nod. "I forgot I had to do somethin' in class, so I'll be headin' off first," she says, giving me a bitter smile.

"Really? But you don't need to rush, right? There's still half of your lunch left."

"It didn't agree with me anyway."

That's definitely a lie. Seiko loves stupidly spicy food like this, and she hates to leave a meal unfinished. Then, this has to be...

"Seiko."I grab her by the wrist, just as she's about to leave.

"W-What?"

"You... forgot your homework again, didn't you?"

"...Excuse me?" Seiko blinks, her mouth hanging open, then she sighs. "...Yeah, sure, you caught me. That's it exactly."

"I knew it." I grin. "I'll give you a hand after school, so don't worry about it and finish your lunch."

"Don't worry?" She makes a face. "Aoi, you..."

"What, not good enough for you? I'll have you know, Tsukasa-chan's been—oh, right! Tsukasa-chan, could you help too? Let's all have a study session together."

"Me?" Tsukasa-chan hesitates for a moment, then gives me a smile. "Of course. I'd... love to."

We all sit back down, and start eating. Tsukasa-chan's seat is facing mine, and we share glances in between bites of our meals. I can feel my heart thump every time our eyes meet; Tsukasa-chan must be feeling the same way, because neither of us can finish a sentence without blushing.

Seiko sighs, rolling her eyes at the two of us, and swallows a spoonful of her 'meal'. Scowling, she turns to Tsukasa-chan. "Well, suppose this is as good a chance as any," Seiko says. "Hiramoto, I'd like to ask you somethin'."

"Yes, Yagami-san?"

"I won't beat around the bush." Seiko sets her spoon down, and looks Tsukasa-chan in the eye. "Just what do you think about Aoi?"

I choke on my ramen. What does Seiko think she's asking!? Opposite me, Tsukasa-chan freezes. "What do I...?"

"Yeah. ...Do you love her? Or—"

"Seiko!" Before she can open her busybody mouth any more, I lean between the two of them and give Seiko a glare.

She scowls right back. "Sorry, Aoi, but I'm serious. Got to do this much, you know? As a best friend. ...Well, take it as a prank if it makes you feel better."

"A prank! In the first place, there are things you can and can't ask, and—"

I'm about to give Seiko both barrels, when Tsukasa-chan cuts me off. "Aoi-chan." I turn to her, and she shakes her head. "...I'm Aoi-chan's girlfriend, after all."

Girlfriend. That one word out of Tsukasa-chan's mouth sends a harpoon through my heart; I slide back into my seat. There's nothing I can say, if she puts it like that.

Tsukasa-chan clasps her hands to her chest, and takes a

deep breath. "Aoi-chan is... To me, she's a prince. I can't put it into words well, but she's strong, and kind, and gentle. I love that Aoi-chan, I've loved her since the first time we met."

Tsukasa-chan is red to the tips of her ears. Considering what she just said, I'd have just spontaneously combusted. As it is, I'm dangerously close.

As for Seiko, though... "Good for you, huh? Aoi. ...I'll be headed back to class first. See you later." She just shovels down the last of her lunch, gets up, and leaves like nothing happened.

* * *

"...See you tomorrow, Aoi-chan."

"Y-Yeah. Bye... Tsukasa-chan."

Waving goodbye to Tsukasa-chan by the school entrance, I watch her disappear back up the stairs, then I collapse against the shoe racks and sigh. Ever since lunch it feels like I've been running a marathon; just looking at Tsukasa-chan makes me remember what she said, and when I do my heart thumps so hard it feels like it'll burst.

...This is all Seiko's fault. What's with her, anyway? She's been so grumpy lately. Sticking her nose in and asking Tsukasa-chan something like that, too! I don't know what she was thinking. And what about Tsukasa-chan? Sure, I'm happy—scratch that, over the moon—but still. She didn't have to take Seiko that seriously.

So... she's loved me ever since the first time we met, huh? That's...

The click of a phone's camera pulls me back to earth. Its owner, a certain trouble-making best friend, sighs. "Aoi. I thought you'd left already."

"Don't scare me like that, Seiko." I scowl at her. "What's with the phone?"

"Oh, this? Nothin', just thought I'd report a disturbance to public morals, that's all."

"What's that supposed to mean?"

"See for yourself." She tosses me her phone, the picture she just took filling its screen, and... do I really grin like that?

Seiko plucks her phone out of my hands, snapping it shut and slipping it back into her pocket. "...Hiramoto?" She asks, raising an eyebrow.

"...Tsukasa-chan had council duties today."

"So you're free."

"...Why?"

"Oh, nothin' much. Just that new restaurant near the old clock tower, and a certain meal you promised me, that's all."

"No way. Not happening, not there. I've seen you eat—nope."

* * *

It's past evening when Seiko and I finish our meal at the old clock-tower, and the streetlights are just coming on as we leave the restaurant.

Seiko stretches, grinning from ear to ear, and gives a contented burp. "Eatin' at a fancy place like that really was somethin', huh? Aoi."

Slipping my—now much lighter—wallet back into my bag, I sigh. "It had better be. I'm going to have to live next month off it."

"Oh, quit complainin' so much. The meal's goin' to go to waste, like that. We had fun, right?"

"...Yeah. It's been ages since we've done something to-gether like this, hasn't it?"

"Someone had to go and get a girlfriend, after all. ...You'd better take Hiramoto out like this sometime, okay?"

"Busybody. I'll bring her someplace even better."

"Oh? Lucky her." Seiko shakes her head. "...I'd better get goin', Unlike some people, I'm busy. See you tomorrow, Aoi." She turns to leave, but—

"Hey, Seiko."

"What?" Looking her impatient best, Seiko turns back to me. Then, she breaks into a grin. Clasping her hands to her chest, she flutters her eyelashes at me. "Aoi-chan, could it be, you...? But, we can't, I mean, you already have Hiramoto-san."

I make a face. "Who's that supposed to be?"

"Who knows. What, talkin' over dinner not enough for you?" She shakes her head again, and sighs. "Let's go some-where we can sit down properly, at least."

There was a park near the clock-tower, so that's where we decided to go. As soon as we arrive, Seiko and I make a beeline for the playground; I take the slide, and she takes the swings. Neither of us have changed a bit from when we were young, as far as our playground preferences go. Not that I can find the energy to get embarrassed about it, when the stars are out and shining so beautifully in the night sky.

"So?" Seiko asks." Just what's got into you, Aoi?"

"I just wanted to hang out a little longer, that's all. ...And I felt a little guilty, I guess."

"Guilty." Seiko arches an eyebrow.

"Well, I've been spending all my time with Tsukasa-chan, right?"

"That's how it goes when you get someone."

"Maybe, but... I just miss when we used to be together all the time, I guess."

"If there's anyone you should be missin', it's your girl-friend."

"Girlfriend... huh?" I try the word out on my tongue; it feels so... strange, unreal even, compared to when Seiko or Tsukasa-chan say it.

Catching the look on my face, Seiko scowls at me. "Aoi, isn't it about time you got serious about Hiramoto?"

I scowl back. "I am serious! And it's none of your business whatever goes on with me and Tsukasa-chan, anyway."

"It's because it's none of my business that I'm tellin' you."
Seiko hops off her swing and marches up my slide, parking
herself beside me. "Up 'til now, have you called her your
girlfriend, even once? ...You love her, right?"

"T-That's... of course I do! I do, but... I mean, look at
Tsukasa-chan, and look at me! She's amazing, and I'm..."

"Aoi, you're such a maiden it's makin' my teeth hurt!"
Seiko gives the slide a smack. "Just how long are you goin'
to enjoy bein' a girl in love?"

"I am a girl in love!"

"You get it by now, right? Remember middle school, Ya-
mada-what's-her-name?"

"...Yeah?"

"You didn't do anythin' because you 'weren't good
enough for her', and what happened?"

"Nothing?"

"Nothin'!"

"...Seiko, are you drunk?"

"No! Now listen, your problem is you're too soft!"

"Soft."

"Dang right you're soft! You got to remember,

Aoi—you're a hunter! If you're serious, then go for the jugular! She who strikes first strikes last!"

"Uh huh. Jugular, got it." Actually, she's starting to make sense. I'm still not convinced she didn't sneak some wine just now, though. It would explain the bill. "So I'm soft. What am I supposed to do about it?"

Seiko stares at me, then she gives the slide another smack. "Figure it out for yourself!"

"...I was an idiot to take you seriously for even a second."

Seiko rolls her eyes, and hops down to the ground like a kid. "What am I, your mom? Now come on, it's getting' cold, so let's hurry up and get goin' already."

I follow her down. "Yes *mother.*"

She's right, though; the wind is starting to pick up, and it's getting pretty cold, even for winter. I guess that's it for tonight.

As I walk home with Seiko, though, something starts to bug me. "Hey. Did I ever tell you about Yamada-san? I thought..."

Seiko sighs. "Even if you didn't say anythin', it was obvious."

"Really?" God, I hope not.

"...Well, guess you could say I had an unfair advantage, figurin' it out."

"What's that supposed to mean?"

"Means you've got a ways to go before understandin' a maiden's heart, that's what."

"A maiden's—you?"

"What else am I supposed to be, chopped liver?"

...I'd say asking that is more than enough answer, personally.

In what feels like no time at all, we reach the bridge where we have to split up. Seiko lives on Tsukasa-chan's side of town, after all.

"...I had fun tonight, Seiko. Let's do this again sometime."

"If you'd ask, I'd be happy to any time." She gives me a small smile. "...Just now's lecture, you'd better take it seriously."

"What, I'm a hunter?"

"No." Seiko scowls at me. "About you, and Hiramoto. You're serious about her, right?"

"Yeah."

"...Then don't mess it up." She doesn't say anything else. Instead—

"W-Whoa, Seiko!?"

She wraps her arms around me in a tight hug, pulling me so close our faces are nearly touching. I mean, it's just Seiko, but still.

"Sorry, doin' something this embarrassin' all of a sudden."

I sigh. "You're hopeless, you know that?"

"...Aoi. You know, I—"

The clatter of aluminum, plastic and glass hitting the sidewalk cuts Seiko off. And, standing behind her is...

"Aoi...chan?"

Tsukasa-chan.

* * *

The three of us—Tsukasa-chan, Seiko and I—are statues, unable to do anything but stare at each other as we stand frozen. Tsukasa-chan is the first to break the silence, with a

55

brittle laugh and frozen smile as she bends down to pick up her fallen telescope. There's a huge crack across its lens, and it matches her expression perfectly.

"Aoi-chan," Tsukasa-chan says, still smiling. "What a coincidence, running into you and Yagami-san together. A late night study session?"

"Hiramoto..." Seiko steps away from me, and reaches out to Tsukasa-chan.

"Yes, Yagami-san?" Tsukasa-chan's voice is like thick, cloying syrup; Seiko looks away, letting her outstretched hand fall to her side.

Tsukasa-chan's turns back to me, her face still that smiling mask. "Yup, I was right," she says. "Aoi-chan, you really are kind. Playing along with me, letting me... letting me make a fool of myself."

I take a step towards her. "N-No, Tsukasa-chan, that's not..."

"Shut up!" She screams, and I stop in my tracks. The mask cracks, and Tsukasa-chan glares at me through the tears welling up in her eyes. "...I should leave you two alone. Goodbye, Aoi-chan," she says, and runs off.

"What am I going to do now?" I groan, letting myself

slump to the ground as I stare off at the direction Tsukasa-chan went.

"Someone like that..." Seiko growls. "Aoi, you don't have to do anythin' for someone like that! ...Just now was my bad, fine. Why are you the one she gets angry at?"

"...I'm her girlfriend, after all." Seiko turns her glare on me. I return it with a weak smile. "I thought I'd try listening to what you said, that's all."

"After seein' her like that? When she won't even bother to hear you out?" My eyes widen; I've never seen Seiko so angry. Catching my look, she just shakes her head. "...It's nothin'."

"When you're that worked up?"

"...I'm just disappointed, that's all. That... idiot doesn't even realize how lucky she is, and she goes and does somethin' like this. ...Hey, just forget about her. After seein' how she was just now... she's not good enough for you!"

"Seiko! Don't talk about Tsukasa-chan that way."

"I will! She's not lookin' at you at all, Aoi! She can talk pretty all she likes, but if this is how she is..."

Seiko's words slam home like gunshots, and I growl. "...It isn't any of your business anyway, so just leave me alone. I love her."

"Yeah?" Seiko snarls. "Well, I love you, you idiot!"

The boiling anger inside me freezes in an instant. "Seiko...?"

She pales, and takes a step away from me.

"Seiko... just now, what did you..."

"...Sorry, Aoi. I guess I must have had some alcohol after all. I-I'd better go."

Seiko doesn't say another word; she just turns around and dashes off. I can't do anything, but watch her leave.

* * *

Collapsing into my bed, I glare at my phone's display. "Send something back already!"

How long has it been since I got back? It feels like days. Both Seiko and Tsukasa-chan haven't replied to a single one of my messages. I give up, and throw the useless lump of plastic aside, then I just bury my face in my pillow and scream. It's not like it does any good, but I have to do something or I'll explode. If they'd just pick up! As it is, everything I do just—

I'm interrupted by the insistent beeping of my ring-tone.

Scrambling to pick it up, a quick look at the display nearly makes me drop the phone again: it's Tsukasa-chan.

"H-Hello!? Tsukasa-chan! About just now—"

"...Aoi-chan." Her voice is trembling, so much I can tell even over the phone.

"Tsukasa-chan...?"

"Hey, Aoi-chan. Let's break up."

"W-What are you talking about, Tsukasa-chan?"

"Don't pretend, Aoi-chan. What were you doing with Yagami-san today?"

"Nothing! We just went out for a meal, and—"

"And then you decided to let her kiss you."

"No! Seiko wouldn't do something like that!"

"...So you're going to take her side."

"What 'side' are you talking about? I just..."

"Aoi-chan. The truth is you love Yagami-san, right? Not... not me."

"Of course not!"

"Liar." Her voice slips like a knife of ice into my heart.

"Please, believe me, Tsukasa-chan! I—"

"I will. I will, if you never speak to her again."

"...What? Tsukasa-chan, what did you just..."

"If you stop being friends with Yagami-san, then I'll believe you. You love me, right? Aoi-chan. Then..."

"Don't be ridiculous. Never speak to Seiko again? Because I love you? You've got to be kidding. How can you even ask me that? Apologize to her, right now."

"I won't! In the first place—!"

"In the first place what? You wouldn't even bother hearing me out? You made me have a fight with my best friend!"

"Aoi-chan...?"

"...Fine then. If throwing Seiko away is what it takes to prove I love you, then maybe I don't!"

"Wait! I, I didn't—"

"Goodbye, Tsukasa-chan."

I hang up.

"Tsukasa-chan, you idiot!" I scream at the top of my lungs. It makes my throat hurt, but at least it makes me feel a little better.

...That's a lie. I feel horrible. I bury my face in my pillow. I'm crying. My eyes are burning, my face is burning, and it hurts to breathe.

"Tsukasa-chan... you idiot."

* * *

"Aoi? Aoi, are you in?"

I wake up to the sound of someone knocking on the door, downstairs. Crawling out of bed, I look at my alarm clock. It's... three in the morning? I yawn. Who could it be at this hour? I just got to sleep, too... Oh, wait. Orange, afternoon light is streaming in from under my curtains. I overslept...?

For now, though, I need to get the door. Stumbling my way down the stairs, I make my way to the door just in time to hear a familiar sigh.

"Figures, she isn't here."

I pull the door open, to reveal Seiko, with her hands on her hips and her usual scowl firmly in place.

"What, you were in? The teach made me drop by, since you didn't call, but..." She trails off, and looks me over.

"I just woke up, okay?"

"Everythin' alright?"

"...None of your business."

"Oh, I see. Guess it can't be helped, then—not. Like I could just leave you like this. Come on, let me in already." Without waiting for an answer, Seiko just pushes me aside and barges in.

Seiko starts on a pot of tea, then she sends me back to my room to wash up, at least. By the time I crawl back into the living room, the tea's already cold. She pours me a cup anyway, and sits down opposite me.

"...You're being nice today," I say, staring into the tea's murky depths.

Seiko glares at me. "What's that supposed to mean? I'm always nice."

"...Yeah, you are."

"Well, you know, I couldn't just leave you alone like this."

"...Thanks." I take a slow sip from my cup; the tea might be cold, but it's warm. So warm, just a sip of it makes my eyes start to burn. Seiko's really something—even after last night, she's still... her.

"What happened?" Seiko eventually asks, after we've sat there for who knows how long.

"We... Tsukasa-chan and I, we fought, last night. I, I..." I can't continue, the tears welling up in my eyes stopping me.

Seiko gives me a small smile, and takes my hand in hers. "Calm down, Aoi. Tell me everythin', from the beginnin'."

* * *

Seiko leans back in her chair and crosses her arms. "I see."

"Well?"

"You two are terrible."

"I... I don't know if I'd go that far—Tsukasa-chan was pretty worked up, and she probably didn't—"

"Her, yeah, but you too, Aoi. I don't like her, but you do, right? Then what are you doin', takin' my side?"

I scowl. "So, what? 'I'm sorry I had a best friend before meeting you, let me fix that?' "

"Pretty much, yeah. You remember last night, right? I was cheatin', no two ways about it. If Hiramoto hadn't come when she did, I really would have..." Seiko shakes her head. "All this time, I've been sayin' I'd cheer you on when

I've really been wantin' you for myself. What I said about her last night proves it. ...I'm a failure of a friend, Aoi."

"That's not true!" I take her hands in mine. "Nothing actually happened, right? And you only said those things because you were worrying about me!"

"Sure, I was worryin'. But not as your best friend."

"That... it doesn't matter."

"So you're fine with me as your girlfriend, then?"

Seiko's words cut at me like a knife; I can't meet her eyes.

"Yeah, I thought so. You really do... love her, after all. I hate to admit it, but she probably feels the same way about you."

"What am I supposed to do now, then?"

"Go apologize. I'll go home, and from tomorrow mornin' on, we'll just be normal classmates. Nothin' to fight about then, right? Everythin's solved, everyone's happy."

"Are you serious? Seiko, you're seriously saying that?"

"...Yeah."

"Don't be ridiculous! There's no way I can do that! We're sisters, got it?" I stand up from my chair and grab Seiko by the shoulders. "I can't just... throw you away. I won't."

64

"I would. If I was you and you were Hiramoto, in a heart-beat."

"You wouldn't have a best friend."

"My job, then."

"You're lying. Comics are your dream."

"I'm serious. What, are you just playin' around? You're serious about her, right?"

"That's... this and that are..."

"This is what the real world is like, Aoi. Or, what? Are you goin' to dump her, then? Give up?"

I can't answer. Last night, I would have. I did. Seiko isn't wrong, either. That's what the world is like, I'm sure. You can't have your cake and eat it, right? And love is all about sacrifice, isn't it? That's what they all say. Then is this love, or just a crush? I...

"No. You're wrong, Seiko."

She narrows her eyes into a glare. "Aoi..."

"Yeah. It's a little different for me, but I love you too. But, you're wrong. If love is like that, then I'm fine playing.

That kind of 'love' is too painful."

"So do you love her or not?"

"I... I don't know. But I want to believe I do. I don't want to leave things between us like this. ...And, you know, got to strike first, right?"

Seiko leans back and takes a long, slow breath, then she breaks into a bitter grin. "So you do understand a maiden's heart, a little."

I grin right back at her. "I'm a girl in love, after all."

* * *

I don't even bother getting my phone, as I rush out the house. Tsukasa-chan's home is nearly an hour away on foot, way too far as it is. And I don't even know what I'm going to do when I get there! But all that can wait. For now, I run into the back-yard and make a beeline for the shed. Where is that old—there it is!

Standing where it's been for the last two years or so is my old bike. I hop on, and start pedaling. Thank god, it still works. It's covered in rust, and the last time I used it I was about six inches shorter. The tires are weird, too, soft and squishy from the air leaking out, or something. I don't care.

"Seiko! Take care of the house!"

"Yeah, yeah. Leave everythin' to me." She sends me off, an exasperated scowl on her face and my abandoned phone in hand.

I pedal as fast as I can. It's way harder than I remember—the rust and tires make it like pushing a boulder up a slope. Less than two minutes in, my back starts to hurt like anything. I make it to Tsukasa-chan's house in twenty minutes flat.

Parking my bike, I hop off, Okay, I'm here—now what? But, Tsukasa-chan answers that question for me, when her door flies open to reveal her standing in the doorway, the phone she was holding tumbling to the floor. My eyes widen in shock—don't tell me, Seiko...

Tsukasa-chan gasps. "Aoi-chan!? You really came!"

I shake my surprise off, and give Tsukasa-chan a shaky smile, the best I can do. "...Of course I did. I'm... your prince, after all."

"Aoi-chan!" Tsukasa-chan runs to me, throwing herself into my arms. She's crying and, I realize, so am I. "I'm sorry!" she sobs. "I-I'm so sorry! I—"

"Me too. So, please, let me go first. I... I was stupid, getting worked up like that. I won't apologize for what I said, but..." I take a deep breath. When I look into her eyes, I can see myself reflected inside—it gives me the last push I need. "I'm sorry, Tsukasa-chan. Even if you ask me to prove I love you, there's not much I can say. About the only thing I can do is..."

Leaning in, I bring my lips to hers. The moment we touch, my mind erupts in glorious fireworks, and I tighten my arms around her. After a moment, she does the same to me. Our kiss lasts for a blissful eternity, and when our lips part we're both breathing hard.

"Aoi-chan..."

"...Tsukasa-chan. You said you fell in love with me the first time we met, but... I've been in love with you from the moment I first saw you. I love you, Tsukasa-chan, more than anyone else in this world. Will you go out with me?"

fin

nostalgia fragrance

I hate the smell of autumn. Dead leaves and smoke, burning—I can't stand them. Every day is like a funeral, the stink of ash sticking to my clothes, my hair. It makes me remember. A long time ago, when the air smelled just like this, I lost someone very important to me.

"You really aren't very cheerful this time of year, huh? Ann."

Next to me at our store's register, my co-worker Kuroe sends a small smile my way. As usual, we've just been standing here with nothing to do. Just another day in fair Southlight city.

"I'm surprised you noticed." It's only been two years working together. I thought I had a better poker face than that.

"You don't have to be that way." She sticks her tongue out at me.

"I was born this way."

"I mean, you could be a little nicer."

"I thought you preferred me like this."

"It was just a little question."

"...I hate this season, that's all."

"Ann?"

"No. I didn't say anything. Really."

* * *

With the end of another work day, I emerge from the store's back door to find Kuroe waiting for me. Rarely enough, our shifts ended at the same time today. Our manager almost never lets this happen, thank goodness. I'd be happier without the almost.

"Hey, Ann, do you want to stop by someplace? There's a teashop by the station I've been dying to try, and, if you'd like..."

To her credit Kuroe doesn't let that friendly mask of hers slip an inch. Combined with the stink of autumn in the air, it's oppressive.

"There's a show I need to catch."

"...That's a lie, right?"

"What makes you say that?"

"You don't watch TV. Even when we were in school to-gether—"

"School? What's that, something to eat?" I don't know what she's talking about. And even if I did... "People change. Right now I'm just a normal twenty-one-year-old hooked on dramas. Really."

"You don't change a bit, Ann."

"I could say the same about you."

Kuroe puts a finger to her lips and looks up at the sky as she walks, the picture of a young girl deep in thought. I'm quite envious—only eighteen and she's already mastered the art of walking in high-heels, not even needing to look where she's stepping. If I did something like that I'd trip and fall before I even put them on.

After walking like that for a while, she turns to me with a smile. It doesn't look put on in the least. "...I don't think that's true, Ann. I've changed a lot since you graduated. Ah, of course, what I told you that day hasn't changed, one bit. Even now, I—"

"I forgot, I have somewhere I need to be." Cutting Kuroe off, I turn around and start walking away.

"See you tomorrow!" But, she calls out a goodbye to me anyway. I don't bother responding.

* * *

"Good afternoon, Ann."

"...Afternoon."

When I arrive at work, Kuroe is already standing behind her register. Worker bees could learn a thing or two from her. Just another thing that hasn't changed in the three—or was it two, I forget—years I've known her.

Be it studies, sports, or work, Kuroe always gives a hundred and ten percent. Speaking as someone who's had to work with her for two years, I can say that her earnestness is understandable within a minute of meeting her. It's as if she's flaunting it, rubbing it into the face of anyone around.

Taking my place beside my own register, I start setting everything in order. There isn't a single customer, or any chance of one coming, but as long as I'm getting paid I need to do at least this much. What a pain, really. And, even though our shop is air-conditioned, every breath I take is filled with the smell of autumn. It mixes with Kuroe's sweet perfume to form a choking miasma. I feel light headed.

"I really do... hate this season."

"Did you say something, Ann?"

"No."

72

The day stretches on. A minute turns into ten, ten into sixty.

"Nobody's coming, huh?" Playing with one of the knick-knacks we have lying around, Kuroe cranes her neck to look outside. Crowds of people are just passing us by.

"As usual."

"Won't it be a problem? If there aren't any customers."

"We'll just close down."

"No way! If that happens, we won't be able to work together any more!"

"You'll find a better job."

"What about you?"

"Who knows?"

"Why do you have to be like that?"

"I promised my mother I wouldn't talk to strangers."

"We've known each other three years!"

"Oh, you're right." I put a hand to my mouth, in shock. I had completely forgotten. It's really two, though. "...Well, I'll probably go overseas."

"Really?"

"Really."

"No way!" Kuroe's eyes widen in shock. It looks perfectly natural. Maybe I should get her to teach me how to act like that. "Then? What are you going to do? Transfer to a university there, or..."

"My father wants me to take over his company on Wall Street."

"That's just another lie, isn't it?" She scowls at me. How irresponsible—what if she got a wrinkle? "You told me your dad was an actor."

"I did? Then that was a lie too."

"You're kidding."

"It's true. Really. Actually, I'm an orphan. Also, I'm really in my thirties."

"Seriously!?"

For the first time in my life, I see someone jump into the air in shock—or pretend to, at least. Talk about overacting.

"Kya!"

...And for the first time, I see someone proceed to trip over themselves and fall. Kuroe tumbles, her head on a collision course with the corner of the register, and—

"Kuroe!"

Luckily enough for her, I just happen to be walking over when it happened. As they say: when it rains blessings, it pours. What a lucky girl, for someone so careless. Or is it foolish, considering she brought it on herself in the first place? Well, children and fools...

"Thank you, Ann. You saved me." From within my arms, Kuroe sighs in relief.

"...Really? I hadn't realized. I'm so sorry."

She sighs again, heavier this time. Was it something I said? "I just wanted to thank you."

"I don't remember doing anything to be thanked for. Or is this about my lending you money for cab fare? You're welcome."

"Do you have to be like that?"

"No, but if I don't tell the truth I'll die." This close to her, my head is full of Kuroe's perfume. It floods my senses, making my vision swim. I'm surprised there's a market for an oppressive smell like this.

I try to get away from her, but Kuroe grabs onto my sleeve and doesn't let go. "In that case, thank you. For calling my name."

What a bourgeois—no, bohemian?—girl. As if that meant anything. In the first place, I didn't. Really.

"I need to get back to my register." I shake her hand off. But, her scent doesn't let go so easily. It hangs around my neck like a noose, even stronger than the smoky stink of autumn. My arms are limp, my body hollow, and it's as if I'm seeing everything once removed.

"Oh. ...That's right. Come... to think of it..." Floating inside myself as I am, I start remembering all sorts of nasty things. "...The...first time we met..."

"Ann?" Kuroe sends a worried look my way. I barely notice, my vision is wobbling so much.

"...it was... like..."

Ah. I must have really pushed myself. Even if it was just an accident, I shouldn't have bothered. At least not on an empty stomach. Thanks to all the blood rushing to my head, there isn't any left for little things like not fainting. What a miscalculation. Even though this season is hard enough on me as it is...

"Ann? Are you all right?"

I really do—

"Ann!"

* * *

What a nostalgic smell. Two years... This is the perfume she used to wear, lilies in full bloom. Sinking into that sweet fragrance, I let myself dissolve.

"...Mother...?"

I wake up in our store's break-room. Blinking my eyes against the harsh fluorescent white light, I look around. The clock tells me I haven't been asleep long, at least. As I try to prop myself up, though, my vision fills with Kuroe's face. She's... crying.

The moment our eyes meet, hers open wide. "Ann! You're awake?"

"...No, I'm not."

"Liar."

"It's true. I'm just very good at talking in my sleep."

"No way, really?"

"Really."

"Then I guess I'd better not believe anything you tell me."

"Exactly."

"You look pretty happy for someone who just collapsed."

"I had a nostalgic dream."

"Was it a happy one?"

"Very."

"You should smile more often. You look prettier this way."

"You should cry more often. You're beautiful with tears in your eyes."

"Then you should say nicer things."

"To our manager?"

"You're that way even asleep, huh."

"I don't know what you're talking about."

"You lie just as much too."

"I was born like this."

"...You know, I was happy."

"Because I collapsed? Now who's the mean one?"

"You might be right."

I'm actually asleep now. Really. That's why I didn't hear her laugh—not how it sounded like the chiming of beautiful bells; not how it made her face seem to glow, a rainbow through the tears still filling her eyes. I didn't notice a single one of those things. Not at all.

"Kuroe... do you like this season?"

"Of course."

"Why?"

"Hmm, I wonder."

"You really are mean."

"Not as much as you, Ann. How about you then? The way you're smiling, it doesn't look like you hate it as much as you say."

"No."

I shake my head, still asleep.

"I hate autumn. All of it. Most of all, the smell."

"Really?"

"No, not really."

I can still smell Kuroe's perfume. It's the sweet scent of lilies. If I was awake I'd have to get away, I hate the smell so much. But I'm asleep right now so it can't be helped.

"...My shift?"

"The manager took over for us. Why, did you want to get back to work?"

"I'm sleeping well now."

"Then I guess it can't be helped. Sweet dreams, Ann."

fin

Infirmary Heart

When I was young, I thought doctors and nurses could fix anything. As I grew older, though, I realized that was just my naivety speaking. So why is it that, at seventeen years old, I'm in the school infirmary looking for the cure to a broken heart?

"Kazumiya Izumi?"

Looking up from the papers on her desk, the school nurse Yoshida-sensei gives me a smile. "From the third year, correct? Now, where are you feeling unwell today?"

Looking into her chestnut eyes I feel five-years-old all over again, faking a stomachache to get out of school. I bite my lip. "I'm... a little anemic. Fujisawa-sensei gave me permission to rest."

"I see."

I feel like a pane of glass under her gaze, but she doesn't say anything else. She just keeps smiling that gentle smile, looking at me with those kind eyes. And here I am, lying to such a kind person, all because I'm a spoiled brat who can't deal with her problems herself. Sensei's eyes are kind—so much so, they make my chest ache.

"Um... I'll just lie down, so..."

"Sure. But, you know..." Yoshida-sensei lays her hand over mine. "If you're feeling up to it, how about I get you something to drink? Just lying down until lunch would be pretty boring, wouldn't it?"

"I... I guess?" I don't know what else to say, so I just nod instead.

"Great. I'll be right back."

Yoshida-sensei gets up from her chair and heads for the door. As she leaves, she flashes me a smile—it turns the clock back years. I'd always thought of her as an adult, whenever I saw her at school events or assemblies, but that smile makes her look more like a mischievous older student. It makes her eyes sparkle.

Yoshida-sensei is gone from the infirmary for only a few minutes; when she comes back, it's with two steaming mugs of coffee.

"Here you go." Setting one mug down in front of me, she takes a slow sip from the other.

"Um... thank you."

"Don't worry about it, I was just getting thirsty anyway.

Do you like yours with sugar? Cream?" Yoshida-sensei gestures at several paper sachets, all standing upright in a mug on her desk.

"...No, I take my coffee black"

"Oh? I'm surprised. I can't stand mine without sugar."

"Really?"

"I can't take the bitterness, otherwise. Is it that surprising?"

"N-No! I just thought, black seemed to fit Yoshida-sensei's image, so..."

"I don't know about that." She laughs. "Oh, and you can stop being so formal. It's only the two of us here, so just call me Ami."

"But..."

"It must be tiring, right? Being so stiff."

"...Okay. Um, Ami-sensei...?"

"That's the spirit. Isn't that better? I'll call you by your name too, if you don't mind."

"...I don't."

"Well then, Izumi-san. Since we're chatting, is there anything in particular you want to talk about?"

Oh. "...I'm anemic."

"Hmm, anemia, huh? Anemia, anemia, anemia." Ami-sensei grins at me, her eyes laughing. She's teasing me!

"Um, Sensei, I think I'd better..."

She puts her hands up, heading me off. "Don't worry, Izumi-san, I won't pry. How about I start, then. Is there anything you want to ask me?"

"Um, well..." To be honest, not really. But, if it's just something I'm curious about... "Then... Ami-sensei... some of the girls in class were saying you went to school here, but..."

She chuckles. "That's right, I'm an alumnus of this school."

"Really? You studied here?"

"Of course. It was before your time, though." She pauses, giving me a mischievous grin. "Would you like to guess how long?"

"Ami-sensei, that's..." Unfair. Before I finish speaking, though, I stop myself. Somehow, it feels like I'll have lost if I say that. Instead... "Um... six years ago, maybe?"

"Oh? I'm flattered. It was seven, actually." Sensei's smile is an electric live-wire, as she laughs. "Thank goodness you didn't say ten, or twenty. I might have had a heart attack."

"There's no way I would! You're still young, Ami-sensei! It's almost like you're not a teacher!"

Ami-sensei freezes mid-sip, then she bursts out laughing.

"Sensei!?"

"No, it's nothing, don't mind me. ...Ah, yes, at your age, that's how it is, isn't it. I was like that too. But you'd better not say that where any of the other teachers can hear, Izumi-san."

"Huh? Why would..." Oh. W-What did I just say!? I didn't mean it like that! I open my mouth to apologize, but Ami-sensei stops me with a finger to my lips.

"Don't worry, Izumi-san. I understand—I did say I was the same, didn't I? You didn't mean anything disrespectful by it, right?"

"N-No! I-I mean, I didn't! Mean it, that is." I nod, pause, then... "That is! I meant what I said about you being young, but—!"

"You're a cheerful girl, aren't you? Izumi-san." Ami-sensei's smile is gentle, and her brown eyes dance as she chuckles. She takes another long sip from her mug, then she nods. "Well, that's a little about me. How about you, Izumi-san? Anything you want to talk about? Problems, maybe?"

"I..."

"Ah, right. I say you, but if there are any problems any of your friends might have, feel free to ask for them too."

"Y-Yes! That's right! ...I-I mean, I do. Have a friend with a problem."

"Oh? That's not good. What kind of problem?"

"Well, the thing is, she has a... girlfriend."

"I see. Isn't that a good thing?"

"It is! It is, but... but lately, she and her girlfriend are, you know, quarreling. About next year. They're both third-year students, like me, and they're graduating. Like me. But, her girlfriend is going to a university in Tokyo. And I—I mean, she can't."

"She can't? Because of her grades?"

"No... she doesn't want to make her parents spend that kind of money. The course she wants to attend is local, too."

"I see. That sounds like it might be a problem."

I bite my lip, as I remember our last fight. "I... I'm starting to think she doesn't care about me, not as much as that university of hers."

"Really? I don't think that's necessarily true, though? You—your friend is in a tough spot right now, but I think her girlfriend might be in one too."

"Really? M-My friend, that is. And her girlfriend, they're like that?"

"I can't say for certain, of course. They've been together for...?"

"Two years and six months."

"Two years and a half. So, I'm sure they must care for each other, to stay together so long." Ami-sensei takes a deep breath, sighs, and gives me a sad smile. "But, that's no guarantee they won't split up over this."

"Oh." So Ami-sensei thinks so too.

"Well, I can't say for certain, but..."

"B-But, Ami-sensei, you're an adult, right? Something like this..."

"If only it were that easy. We don't know everything, you know? Especially when it comes to things like love. At times like this... we just try our best." She shakes her head and takes another deep breath. "Well. They might split up, but they might not either."

"Really?"

"It depends on them. All I can say for sure is that dragging it out is definitely worse in the long run. If they just dance around it like this, I'm sure they'll come to regret it in the future."

"But..."

Sensei takes my hands in hers. "However it ends up, you'll need to talk things through seriously. If you fight your way into a breakup, you'll just end up hurting and resenting each other."

For just a moment, Ami-sensei's eyes lose their shine, and I— "A-Ami-sensei! Thank you for the advice! I... I'll be sure to pass it on to them!"

"Oh. ...Well, you're welcome."

There it is, back again, that twinkle in her eyes. Sensei looks so much prettier like this, rather than with that dull, sad brown.

"So, Izumi-san." Sensei gives me a smile, as she finishes off the last of her coffee. "I suppose I should be preparing a bed for you. Unless, maybe you're feeling a little better?"

"I..." I am. "...I'll be fine, Ami-sensei. I'm sorry to have bothered you. I think I can go back to class after all."

Bowing to her, I say my goodbyes and head for the door. Ami-sensei sees me off with a cheerful wave. "Take care. I'll be here if you need me. Or your friends."

* * *

There's not a person around as I make my way to the infirmary; they're all at the school auditorium, for today's morning assembly. Good. Right now, I don't want to talk to anyone at all.

As I arrive in front of the infirmary door, though, I take a deep breath. It's childish of me, I know. But...

Just as I'm about to knock on the door, it slides open. "Oh? If it isn't Izumi-san."

"...Ami-sensei."

"Have a seat." Ami-sensei gestures at the beds in the back of the infirmary. I take one, and she takes the other. Handing me the mug that was on her desk, Sensei gives me a small smile. "Here you go, something to drink. It's mine, but if you don't mind..."

"Thank you, Ami-sensei." Taking it from her, I take a sip. It's lukewarm, and its bittersweet taste sticks in my mouth.

But, I don't dislike it at all.

"So." Sensei steeples her hands and gives me a small smile. "Anemia again?"

"No... My stomach hurts. Fujisawa-sensei let me out of today's assembly."

"I see. ...Things didn't work out?"

"We broke up."

"Oh." Ami-sensei is kind. From her brown eyes to her gentle voice, everything about her is kind. It hurts.

"It's... just like you said. Isn't it? You knew things would end up like this." I can't stand it. Even though, even though it had nothing to do with her, even though it couldn't possibly be her fault, all I can do is say such nasty things.

"I suppose... I thought it was likely." But, she just gives me that smile; without scolding or patronizing me, she just patiently hears me out.

"...Why?" I squeeze my eyes shut, against the pain welling up inside me. "Why aren't you trying to comfort me? Tell me it was just a phase, or that these things never last, or..."

Ami-sensei shakes her head. "Those two years were important to you, weren't they? Then I can't do something like that."

"Ami-sensei..."

Sensei is kind. But, just as much, she's unfair. I didn't cry at all yesterday, but now... the tears well up, and once they start to flow, they refuse to stop. And, like I'm a little girl all over again I fall into her arms, sobbing.

* * *

I must have fallen asleep eventually, because I wake up to the school bell signaling the end of first period. I think. I'm still sleepy, so I can't be sure.

"Are you feeling any better?" Sitting by the side of my bed, Ami-sensei offers me a mug of coffee. It's steaming hot, and it warms me right up.

"...Yes. Thank you, Ami-sensei. I'm... sorry about just now."

"You loved her, didn't you."

For a moment, I feel like breaking down all over again. But, at the same time, wrapped inside Ami-sensei's warmth, my heart feels just a little bit lighter, and I return Sensei's smile with one of my own.

"Yes. I did."

And, the moment I put it into words, the knot of my feelings starts to unravel. I start to cry, warm wet tears flowing down my cheeks.

"I... I really, really did."

"I don't know when, but we drifted apart. It was like she'd become a different person. And... maybe I'd become one, too. I think, maybe we weren't really in love for a while now, we were just telling ourselves we were."

Ami-sensei gives me a small, sad smile. "That's how most relationships end, I think. It just becomes a question of whether you admit it or not. In that respect, Izumi-san, I really do think you're amazing."

When I hear her call my name, my heart skips a beat. It's the same old 'Izumi-san' I've heard quite a bit by now, but something about how she says it is different. Maybe it's how faraway her eyes seem, as if they're gazing at something only she can see.

"...Sensei?"

"Oh! Oh, no, it's nothing. Just... it's nothing."

"I see..."

She gives me a crooked grin. "It really is nothing, you

know? ...Is what I'd like to say, but I suppose it wouldn't be fair if I just left it at that."

"Please! ...I-If you don't mind."

Ami-sensei chuckles, her eyes laughing. "It's fine to be honest, Izumi-san. You're still young, after all."

...She's treating me like a child again!

Sitting back in her chair, Ami-sensei takes a deep breath and sighs. "There's not much to tell, really. I told you I was an alumnus of this school, didn't I? Well, it's a matter of course, but back then there was a different school nurse here. Kanezawa-sensei. And... huh."

"Sensei? What is it?"

"No, nothing much. Just, it's taken me this long to realize I never learned her first name." Ami-sensei laughs, a little sadly, and for a moment I can just see her in my mind's eye, a high school girl like me.

"We wore different uniforms back then, Izumi-san." Sensei winks at me, and my cheeks flush.

"W-Was it that obvious?"

"Just a little. Back then, we wore sailor uniforms."

"Really?"

"Maybe I'll wear the old thing to school one of these days. Give everyone a good scare."

"I... kind of want to see that, actually."

"Why thank you, Izumi-san." Ami-sensei chuckles, and I feel my blush grow even deeper. I didn't mean to say that out loud!

"Now, where were we? Kanezawa-sensei. She was about the same age as I am now, a little younger, maybe? Back then, all I could see was that she was an adult, one I admired. She was the perfect woman, really."

As she talks, Sensei's gaze shifts... somewhere else. The infirmary of seven years ago, maybe.

"I suppose she found me endearing, or maybe just too loud to ignore. At any rate, we became... friends." Ami-sensei gives me a crooked grin. "It didn't last, you know. Certainly not anywhere near as long as two years. I was just a kid, and all I had ever bothered to look at was the 'her' I saw in my mind's eye. I wasn't shy about it, either. It wasn't long before we just... grew tired with each other, and that was that. And now it's just an old story. Bet you regret asking, don't you?"

"Ami-sensei..."

She says it lightly, like it was a joke. But her eyes aren't laughing, not at all. To me, at least, it looked more like she was about to cry.

...I really am a child, after all. I can't find a single word of comfort, or encouragement, or anything. All I can do is sit here and listen.

"Well." Ami-sensei gives herself a shake, and me a smile. "...Are you feeling any better, Izumi-san?"

"Um..." I just feel so small, so pathetic, that I can't even speak properly. Compared to her, I'm nothing.

Yesterday night... hurt. But, even now I still consider Ryuuko a friend, and I think she does too. Seven years from now, we'll still be friends, I'm sure. And yet here I am, letting myself be spoiled by Ami-sensei's kindness. But...

"J-Just a little longer... My stomach... still hurts."

"I see."

She doesn't say anything else. She just gives me that kind smile, and a gentle pat on the head.

* * *

Ever since that day, stopping by the infirmary after school became a habit of mine. I could talk to Ami-sensei about anything: how I want to study our prefecture's art, and take over the family business; that my family wanted me to go to Tokyo and study medicine, law, anything but that. Ami-sensei never laughed at me, or told me I was being silly. She talked to me like I was an adult, an equal. A friend. That infirmary became a second home to me. And, as for Ami-sensei herself...

"Izumi-san, here again?"

Looking up from her usual mug of coffee, Ami-sensei welcomes me into the infirmary with a smile. Her voice practically drips exasperation, but her chestnut eyes sparkle at me.

"Good afternoon, Ami-sensei. I've come again." Stepping into the room, I give her a bow and smile back.

"Will the usual be fine?" Even as she asks, she's already lifting the other mug on her desk and handing it to me.

"Of course. Thank you, Sensei." I wrap my hands around the mug, savoring its warmth. I take a sip, and my smile gets even wider. It's delicious, hot and dark and bitter, with just the tiniest hint of sugar. I call it the Ami-sensei special, but only to myself. "...Sensei, you put sugar in again, didn't you."

"Did I? Oh my. Does it taste bad?"

"It's delicious, like always."

"I'm glad to hear that."

The two of us share a laugh.

Taking my usual seat in the chair beside her, the two of us talk about nothing in particular. How my classes were today, how her work has been piling up with finals around the corner, anything we feel like.

"Have you heard, Sensei? There's an Ouija board boom going on right now. The girls in my class are going crazy over it."

"Ouija board?"

"Um... it's that thing where you write the alphabet on a piece of paper, then..."

"Ah, that. Back in my day, we called it Kokkuri-san. My, but the youngsters nowadays..."

"Geez, Sensei. It hasn't been that long."

"I suppose you're right." Ami-sensei laughs."Well, it's natural for people to start getting interested in things like that, especially now."

"Sensei, you don't believe in that kind of thing?"

"Rather than believing or not, I missed the boat." She gives me a crooked grin. "I always was more of an introvert, after all. And..."

Sensei's eyes lose their shine. From time to time, they go flat, just like this; mostly, when she's talking about her time here in this school.

"It was... around now? That the previous school nurse..."

"Second previous, actually." Sensei chuckles. "She left this school the year after I graduated."

"...Oh."

"I'm surprised you remembered."

"It's... an important memory of yours, after all."

"Maybe at the time. Now..." She waves a hand at the piles of paper cluttering her desk.

What Ami-sensei is saying makes sense. Just three months ago it felt like the world was ending. But... "Then, maybe you're seeing someone else now?"

"Now, why would you ask an old lady something like that?" She arches an eyebrow at me, but then she shakes her head with a chuckle. "I suppose I must have fallen out of falling in love, because she was the first and last."

"Really?"

"Oh? You don't believe me? Adults aren't all about romance, you know?"

"So... you aren't seeing anyone."

I can hear my heartbeat pounding in my ears. It's so loud I'm afraid Ami-sensei's going to overhear.

But, she just gives me a puzzled smile."...No? No, I'm not seeing anyone right now. Why?"

"U-Um..." I force myself to breathe. Deep breaths, in, out, in, out. I can do this—this is my chance! "T-Then... A-Ami-sensei! Please go out with me! I'm in love with you!"

Ami-sensei just stares at me in silence. I can feel myself burning up, from the tops of my ears all the way down to the tips of my toes. Is this how it feels, confessing to someone? I feel transparent, as if Ami-sensei's chestnut eyes can see right through me.

"Hm." Putting her mug back down, Ami-sensei chuckles. "I'm flattered, Izumi-san."

"I-I'm serious, Ami-sensei! I really do—!"

"Thank you, Izumi-san. I meant what I said—I'm flattered, really." Sensei shakes her head. "But, I think you're misunderstanding your feelings. What you're feeling is just admiration. It's perfectly normal, at your age."

"No, that's not... I... I really..." Why...? Why is Ami-sensei saying things like that? Her face is a mask, and while her eyes might be kind, they're just as stern. "Ami-sensei, why won't you believe me?"

"Believe—I do believe you! I just think you're not thinking clearly. I'm an adult, and..."

"I'm not a child!"

"That's what all children say. Adults don't have to."

"What does that make you, Sensei?"

"I... You're a student."

I can feel tears welling up in my eyes. But I do my best, holding them back as I look her straight in the eye. "Then, Ami-sensei, do you hate me?"

"Of course not! I..." She trails off, turning away from me. "Izumi-san, you're still young. It's natural for you to admire someone, but that doesn't mean..."

"...You still haven't answered my question, Sensei."

Ami-sensei's eyes fly open. Her cheeks flush, and she starts to say something, but she bites it back instead. Sensei chuckles, bitterly. "You're much stronger than the day we first met, Izumi-san."

"Then..."

"No."

"...Can I ask why?"

"Before the question of love or... or not, you're a child, a student here, and I'm an adult. I won't accept your confession."

I nod, biting my lip and holding back tears. It's... okay. The moment I decided to confess, I'd prepared myself for something like this. I just never expected it to hurt this much.

"Thank you, Ami-sensei."

"Izumi-san..."

"It's getting late. I had better head home. ...Goodbye, Sensei."

"...Take care. I'll be here if you need me."

* * *

Waving my parents off at the school gate, I weave my way through the crowd back into the building. It's finally graduation day, and all over campus my fellow students are

101

celebrating. After today, we won't be coming back here as students, after all. This is our only chance to really cut loose and enjoy ourselves. As for me, I feel the way I do the night before a test. There are butterflies in my stomach, and my palms are sweating. Walking through the hallways, I make my way to the infirmary.

Along the way, I run into a familiar face. Moritani Ryuuko. A third-year student like me, and a classmate besides. My first love. What a strange feeling. I wasn't sure if I could see her today. I'm glad I did. It was just like Ami-sensei said. We might have gone through a lot, but we're still friends.

I wish her the best for her move to Tokyo, and she gives me one last kiss on the forehead, for luck. We part ways with a smile, something I wouldn't have thought was possible seven months ago, and then I move on.

The hallway leading to the infirmary seems to go on forever. But, in what seems like no time at all, I'm in front of that familiar door. There isn't anyone around, and I start to get a little scared. What if Ami-sensei isn't in? Maybe, maybe she's still at the ceremony, or...

I clasp my hands to my chest and take a deep breath. No, I won't run away. I might have been a child before, but I'm definitely not one now. With my heart thumping in my chest, I knock on the door.

"Come in." Ami-sensei's voice carries clearly through the thin wood door.

Taking another deep breath, I slide it open and step inside. "...Good afternoon, Ami-sensei."

Sensei looks more beautiful than ever, her now semi-long hair up in a neat ponytail and her chestnut eyes framed in a new pair of glasses. She freezes mid-sip, the second our eyes meet, her coffee mug hovering just in front of her lips.

For a moment I'm scared she doesn't recognize me, but then, her stunned expression melts into a smile. "Izumi-san. Congratulations on your graduation."

"Thank you, Ami-sensei."

"Can I get you anything? ...Is what I'd like to say, but the cafeteria is closed today. ...Would you like some of mine?"

"No, I'm fine, Sensei. I don't think I could take anything now."

"...Well then, for now why don't you have a seat?"

Setting her mug aside, Ami-sensei gives me a radiant smile. "Really, I was afraid I wouldn't be able to congratulate you. I thought you might have forgotten me."

"Never, Ami-sensei."

"I'm glad, then. I wouldn't know what to do if you did. Your parents?"

"I just sent them off. I'm meeting them again later, to celebrate."

"I see. ...Looking at you, I'd guess your university courses are settled?"

"Somehow. I managed to qualify for the prefectural scholarship."

"You've really worked hard, haven't you."

"There was... someone I had to catch up to."

"Izumi-san... I..."

"Ami... san. Please."

"...Got it." Sensei closes her eyes, and nods.

"Ami-san, you said it before, right? That I was still a child. Maybe... maybe you were right. Back then, there were so many things I didn't know, so many things I thought I did. These four months, I realized that. And, I learned that when you're doing something for a reason, a real reason, you change, and the world changes too. The one who taught me that was you. My feelings haven't changed, not one bit. I, Kazumiya Izumi, love you, Ami-san."

I can't breathe, my chest is so tight; my hands are shaking, and it feels like I'm about to faint, too. But, at last, I've managed to give Ami-sensei a proper confession.

For what seems like forever, her expression doesn't change. But, eventually she sighs, and that stern mask breaks into a crooked smile.

"Well, I'm beat. I really can't win against you, Izumi-san."

"Ami-san, that means..."

"I was ready to turn you down, you know? I planned it out—how to make sure you weren't hurt, how to make you give up. Everything."

I nod.

"Are you really sure about this?"

"Of course. Asking me that is unfair, Ami-sensei."

"Oh? Back to 'sensei', huh?"

"That's..." I blush.

Sensei's eyes shine bright. "If you're fine with someone like me, I'd be honored. Izumi."

Warmth blooms inside me, a sweet ache that fills me up. The next thing I know, I'm throwing myself into Sensei's arms. "Ami-sensei!"

She just laughs, and wraps me up in her embrace.

* * *

I'm no longer a high school student. I don't have anemia, and my stomach doesn't hurt either. Of course, I can't visit that warm infirmary anymore. But that's okay.

In the middle of spring, in that short period between graduation and the start of my university life, I'm waiting for someone in front of our town's only train-station. Half an hour before the time we agreed on, she arrives. She's back to her old haircut, a short bob, and she's wearing contacts today. That familiar lab-coat of hers is nowhere to be seen. And...

The moment she sees me already waiting, she gives me a crooked grin, her eyes sparkling. "Izumi. It won't be time for our date for a while, you know?"

"Well, what about you then, Ami-san?"

My girlfriend, Yoshida Ami, sighs. "I should have know you'd beat me here. Well, how late am I?"

I laugh. "I just got here myself. ...But, since we're both here, shall we?"

Taking her hand in mine, the two of us start walking.

fin

In the Season of Falling Leaves

"...and I love you all. Yuri."

Panting from the exertion of moving her pen, Kamoda Yuri finished the last sentence of the last letter she'd ever write. She set it, and her too-heavy pen, aside. There, it was done. She stared at that small scrap of paper on her bedside table, the words entrusted to it lined up in clean, neat rows—save for where tears had made the ink run. It was all that would be left of her, after today.

Yuri shifted her gaze to the mug of liquid sitting by her bedside. Her hands trembled, and it hurt to breathe. Well, it hurt more to breathe. She let herself grin one last time. Her now nearly useless muscles had this one last thing to do, and then...

"What are you doing, Yuri?" Finally breaking her silence, the other girl in the room asked.

Yuri started, turning around—and freezing. "Shizuho!? How long..."

"Long enough." Shizuho's expression was an unreadable mask. "What are you doing?"

"...Nothing."

"Really." The other girl walked over, and lifted the mug out of Yuri's reach.

"Wait! Shizuho, don't..."

Shizuho took a sniff. "Alcohol, huh? And your pain pills too, I bet." Shizuho hurled the mug at the far wall; it shattered, spilling Yuri's salvation onto the floor.

"No!" Yuri threw herself forward, reaching for that precious mug, the mug she'd had to spend nearly a day preparing. She barely had time to realize, before she was falling out of the bed.

"Yuri!"

She experienced a moment of weightless escape, then Shizuho's hands were around her, pulling her back.

"No! Shizuho, you don't understand! I, I—!"

Shizuho didn't say a word. She just held Yuri even tighter, so tight Yuri felt like she might break. "...Don't do this to me, Yuri. Please." When she finally spoke, the other girl's voice was a whisper.

Yuri exploded. "Don't do this to you? What about me! I never asked you to do any of this!" She struggled, clawing at Shizuho's arms. "Let me go! I... I don't want to live like this anymore!"

"I do!" Shizuho's voice was hoarse. "I don't want that damn note. I want you here, alive."

"...You're a hypocrite, then. You just want to feel good about yourself, right? That's why you keep clinging on to me like this. You just want me to be your feel-good friend!"

"That's... I've never—*never*—thought of you that way, I swear." Yuri could feel Shizuho trembling behind her. Not from anger, but... Shizuho was crying.

"...Why? Why, then? Why do you keep visiting me like this? When even my own..." Yuri couldn't finish her sentence. She couldn't allow herself to.

"Screw them." Shizuho's voice dropped to a fierce growl, and her arms tightened around Yuri.

"Shizuho... you're hurting me."

"S-Sorry!" Shizuho loosened her hold, but she didn't move away from Yuri. Gently this time, she drew Yuri to her again, wrapping the other girl in her warmth.

"...Why won't you leave, Shizuho?" Yuri finally asked, her voice cracking. "If... if you're going to leave anyway, then leave. It hurts, having you here with me."

"I'm sorry. But I won't leave. Not now, not ever."

"I'm dying, Shizuho. I know it. ...That mug might have been too heavy for me to lift."

"T-That's nonsense! It's just a little... spell. The doctors said—"

"The doctors! It's thanks to them...!" Yuri choked on her words. No. She wouldn't say it, wouldn't admit it. Until the day she died, until after, she wouldn't.

"...So you're just going to lie down like that and die." Shizuho said.

"I don't want to live in a body like this, just wasting away until there's nothing left!" Tears started to pour down Yuri's cheeks. "...I want it to be my choice, at least."

"Don't be selfish! If you die, what happens to... to the people who care about you?"

Yuri laughed, a short, sad bark. "There isn't a single person alive who cares if I live or die!"

"I care! I love you, dammit." Shizuho's words were half shout, half sob. Her hands tightened on Yuri's shoulders, so tightly her knuckles turned white. Yuri winced, a sharp jolt of pain shooting through her; but, even more than that...

"Shizuho...?"

"Don't. Don't say things like that, please. Even if no else on this damn planet does, I do."

"You care about the old me. Not how I am now, a cripple. That's just hypocrisy." Yuri hurled the words at Shizuho like knives. From how the other girl trembled, they hit the mark. Good. At least this way she wouldn't—

"Kya!" With a scream, Yuri landed back down on the bed. And, pinning her down...

"The one I love is you, Kamoda Yuri. You can call it whatever you like. I... I love you." Shizuho kissed her full on the lips. Fever heat swept through Yuri; her eyes opened wide, and she tried to push Shizuho away. But, the other girl didn't budge. Yuri could feel a warmth up against her lips—Shizuho's tongue! It slipped past her teeth, running itself against them, exploring her mouth. She met it with her own, and the two entwined. Yuri could taste Shizuho's gentle warmth, a warmth that made time stand still.

When their lips finally parted, she chased Shizuho's with a gasp. Shizuho's face was flushed, as much as Yuri's must have been, and the two were breathing hard. The sound of their breaths mixed together, the only sounds in the silent bedroom.

Shizuho looked into Yuri's eyes, her own welling up with tears. "Do you believe me now?"

Yuri didn't know what she believed. All she could do was meet the other girl's gentle gaze. "Shizuho... I..."

Shizuho gave her a small, sad smile. "It's okay if you don't believe me. You can even hate me, if you want. But, I want you to live."

The other girl kissed her again—first their lips, then their bodies, melting together in a sweet fever-dance.

* * *

Yuri woke up to the cool morning air; even the still mild early autumn cold was like a knife of winter to her body now, cutting at her even through the sheets. She shivered, and looked around.

Shizuho was sitting by the window, already dressed and watching the scenery outside. Slowly, ever so slowly, Yuri threw her sheets off and sat up, following the other girl's gaze.

Clouds, so much like tufts of cotton, drifted across the crystal blue sky. The sun shone, high up above, and song-birds danced and weaved through the air, their songs an innocent ode to the changing seasons. Even though autumn had barely begun, the trees were already preparing for winter, their leaves dyed red and gold. The outside—Yuri hadn't seen anything like it for nearly a year. She hadn't wanted to.

Yuri's body ached, despite how gentle Shizuho had been. A thick fog of fatigue hung upon her, too. And, she'd never felt more alive, not with the way her heart was overflowing.

"Shizuho." Yuri whispered, into the still morning air.

Shizuho started, standing up and turning around to face her. "Y-Yuri! You're up."

There, on Shizuho's neck, Yuri could see the mark she'd left. The proof she'd been alive. She had its twin. "Good morning. ...Did you sleep well?"

"Y-Yeah." Shizuho didn't look her in the eyes, preferring to let her gaze swim instead.

Yuri smiled. "...Thank you, Shizuho."

"Yuri...?"

"I... I think maybe I'll try. One more time. Could you call the hospital for me?"

"Really!?"

"Yeah. I... I don't want to give up, not yet. Next year, we'll see this scenery again. Together, I promise."

In this season of falling leaves.

114

The Lagoon of Eyes

I was in my cabin, when the storm hit. Even nestled in the depths of the ship, I could feel the waves raging around us. Timber creaked and groaned, and the wind howled like the crescendo of a mad orchestra. I squeezed my eyes tight, against that horrible cacophony, and my hands even tighter.

"Don't worry, Mary." Taking my shivering hands into hers, the other passenger in the cabin with me, my sister Clarissa, gave them a squeeze. "We'll be safe in here. The *Bastion* is a fine ship, and the captain is a good man."

I shook my head, and gave her a shaky smile. "I'm fine, Clarissa, really. This is... I'm just being silly."

"It can't be helped. Not after what happened to Mother." Clarissa's hands trembled, nearly as much as mine did.

A peal of thunder split the air, and we flinched as one. The storm was getting stronger, and the wood around us groaned. Clarissa's grip on my hands tightened. And then, the world shattered in electric light and deafening thunder.

The cabin wall exploded inwards, sending a storm of wood splinters flying. We screamed, as one, as seawater rushed in through the rent hull, hands of ocean brine snatching us away into the depths of the sea.

The water was icy cold, a chill that pierced the thin underclothes I wore to cut at my very being. For a single mad moment we clung to each other, Clarissa and I, plumes of crimson erupting into the water where our desperate clawing had drawn blood.

That second lasted an eternity. The next, and our frozen time began to move once again. Churning water buffeted us, tearing Clarissa and I apart; the ocean's greedy claws wrapped around me, tearing me away from my sister.

I remember her hands, reaching for me, her mouth open in a soundless scream. Then, the ocean closed in around me, and I knew nothing else.

* * *

I awoke to the warmth of the afternoon sun, and a cold stone floor against my back.

Where...? Sitting up, I took in my surroundings. Surrounded by impassive walls of smooth gray-blue stone, I was certainly nowhere near my warm cabin aboard the *Bastion*. In front of me was the cave mouth, a sheer drop down into the sea beyond; behind me was a large tunnel that must lead deeper in. But, deeper in where?

No, before that—how did I get here? Did I wash up, after last night? But... there hadn't been land for miles. T-Then, maybe...

No, no, no! I shook my head, fierce as I could, casting the thought out of my mind. But its icy grasp refused to loosen from around my heart, and I wrapped my arms around myself and shivered against it, and the wind's sudden chill.

...Shivered. Shivered!

Relief flooded me, coursing through my veins to erupt from my mouth as maniacal laughter. Shivering! I could shiver—I was alive!

Eventually, my hysteria faded. With it went that rush of insane energy, leaving me with nothing but my thoughts for company.

It was ridiculous—all I could think about was the state of myself. My simple cotton camisole and bloomers, now the only two pieces of clothing to my name, were utterly inundated with seawater. They clung to me with damp tenacity, like a second skin, a sickly sweet miasma of brine and decay hanging over them. My hair wasn't any better. Caked with sea-slime, it resembled not so much my usual curls as a particularly filthy mop—one that had recently been in a fight with the sea, and lost.

I had to laugh. I was obsessing over how I looked, felt, when by all rights I should be dead! There were a thousand other things I could, should, be doing now, like finding food and shelter, or help, or, or—!

Or Clarissa.

I collapsed to the cave floor, a marionette with her strings cut. And, like a baby, I just sobbed her name over and over again.

* * *

I must have fallen asleep on that cold stone floor, crying for my sister, because the next thing I know my head is on someone's lap, their gentle hands stroking my hair.

"It's going to be all right, you're safe now." They—she?—whisper. Her voice is kind. I can't make out her face, through the tears still staining my vision.

I try to say something, anything, but only sobs pass my lips. Her embrace tightens, her warmth flooding into me. "You must have been scared, waking up alone. I'm sorry. I shouldn't have left you like that."

Ah, I know this feeling. This is just like... "Sister...? Is that you?" Finally, I find my words. My voice trembling, I reach out with uncertain hands, searching for her face. "You're... Clarissa, aren't you?"

Her hands freeze around me, for an instant. Then, she tightens her embrace, so much it feels like I might break. And, in a tear-stained voice...

"...I'm sorry. I'm so, so sorry. I'm... I'm not your sister."

"My name's Yulia, Yulia LeRoux," she says, as she helps me to my feet.

"I am Mary Arkham. ...You saved me, didn't you? Thank you."

Yulia shakes her head, her tanned cheeks flushing. "I happened to see you floating by while I was fishing, that's all. I'm sure you'd have done the same thing."

"Please don't say that." I give her a shy smile. "I can't swim."

"That would be a problem, wouldn't it." Yulia laughs. "...At any rate, I'm glad you're up. You've been asleep since I found you. I was afraid you were never going to come to. ...For now, follow me. Let's get you something to eat."

"Oh. Yulia, do you live nearby?" So I did wash up on land, thank God! But, as if giving the lie to my sudden relief, Yulia's expression clouds.

119

"No, I... I live in a fishing village on the coast."

"...So we're taking a boat." I shiver, at the thought, but steel myself against it. What else am I going to do, stay here the rest of my life?

Instead of answering me, though, Yulia's gaze swims. And then, in a voice heavy as lead, she says: "I... don't have a boat. Not any more."

"What... what are you saying, Yulia? Please, don't tell me..."

"I washed up here, on this island, during a storm. I've been stuck since then. And, now... you are too. I'm... sorry."

"No..." I shrink, inside myself. The world seems to spin around me, and black spots dance on the edges of my vision. I, I—!

"Hey, calm down, Mary." Yulia places her hand on my shoulder, pulling me back from that black precipice. "Don't worry, everything's going to be all right. Chin up."

"But—!"

"Later." Yulia cuts me off with a firm shake of her head. "It's no good worrying about that now, not when you must be starving. Let's get you something to eat first, okay?" Once again, she offers me her hand.

"I…" Inside me swirls a whirlpool of terror and panic and last night and the *Bastion*, a black morass that'd swallow me up, if I let it. I'm sure, if I don't take Yulia's hand, I'd never be able to move from this spot again. So, with as brave a smile as I can force, I do.

"…You're right. Thank you, Yulia. …Let's go?"

* * *

Leading me by the hand, Yulia takes me deeper into the tunnels that, according to her, honeycomb the island. After a short walk, we emerge into a huge cavern, one wide enough for a ballroom, easily, and high enough to fit a small house.

Dominating one end of the cavern was a large, flat rock; the other sank into a pool of water fed from a crack in the cavern wall. What struck me the most, though, was the light. The cave walls shone, with a light as bright as the morning sun and blue as a lake on a clear summer day. It seeped into me, stealing at least some of the uncertainty I felt and replacing it with a sense of… comfort, of home.

I'm utterly captivated. "This… this is amazing, Yulia."

She grins. "I know. It's beautiful, isn't it? And all this light, from just one little hole up there, too."

"Hole?"

"Look." Yulia points up, at the cavern ceiling. Sure enough, there it is, at the very apex of the ceiling's dome; a hole so tiny—about as wide as my arms stretched out, or the size of an attic window—I'd have never noticed it was there.

"...So that's why it's so bright in here."

"Hard to believe, right? More importantly though, here." Yulia leads me to the cavern's large rock.

"Here?" I frown, lost. There's nothing on the rock but some rags, a knife, and a small pile of... fish.

"Tonight's dinner." Yulia offers me one of them and, not knowing what else to do, I take it. There's a neat hole in its side, gleaming rusty-red with piscine blood, and the *thing* is still twitching.

A shiver runs down my spine, as my gaze meets the fish's unblinking eyes; Yulia's expression turns apologetic, as she takes mine in.

"I'm sorry, Mary, but... I've been here for days, and I haven't seen a piece of wood larger than a stamp. And, well, there's nothing else to eat, so..."

The fish is still moist with seawater in my hands, its scales prickling at my palms. I wonder how it would taste? Raw, probably. Would it be slimy? Or maybe soft, and mealy? I'd have to bite into this, feel its still-shivering flesh on my tongue, taste its bitter blood. I don't even like fish.

"Mary?" Yulia leans over, to look up into my eyes. "...Are you okay?"

"I..." I pause. Then, taking a deep breath, I nod. "Yes, I'm fine." That's right. I won't be defeated here, by a *fish* of all things.

In the end, I couldn't stop at just one fish. No matter how much I hated the sensation of it in my mouth, my stomach was honest. I'd never realized just how hungry a person could get.

Choking down the last of my meal, I run to the cave pool—our only source of fresh water, according to Yulia—and drown the taste of fish with as much water as I can stomach. It's only when my mouth is clean once again, the nausea welling up inside me fading, that I heave a small sigh of relief.

"Feeling a little more alive now?" Tossing the remains of her own meal aside, Yulia asks with a gentle smile.

I nod. "I'm ... still not used to the taste, though."

She laughs. "I know what you mean. It's not really something you'd do, if you had a choice. Certainly not at home."

"...You mentioned your home before, too. You said you washed up here, but, how...?"

Yulia laughs, bitterly. "It's not a story worth telling. I got into a stupid argument with my Pa, stupidly took a boat out to sea in a storm, and here I am."

"Oh. ...I'm sorry, Yulia."

"No, it's fine." Yulia gives me a grin. "Chin up, right? Everything's going to be all right. More importantly, now that we've finished dinner, how about I show you around the island? Or, the tunnels, at least. There isn't much time before night falls, but we can get in a bit, I'm sure." Standing up, Yulia offers me her hand. I take it.

"Thank you, Yulia. I'll be in your care."

"Leave it to me."

* * *

"...By the way, Mary," Yulia suddenly asks, as she leads me through the tunnels. "Your sister... um, Clarissa, was it? What does she look like?"

I freeze mid-step. A wave of nausea rises up inside me, from the pit of my stomach to the back of my mouth. The world around me dims; the ground spins, and my vision shakes.

"...Mary?" Yulia's voice fills with worry. "If... if it's too hard for you to talk about, then never mind. I shouldn't have asked."

"No, don't worry about it, Yu...lia?" I look up at her, re-assurance on my lips. But, where her face should be is instead a blank expanse, a shapeless mask of flesh.

The world screeches to a halt. I bite down on the scream that fights to escape my mouth, shaking my head and squeezing my eyes shut. No, no! I'm... I'm seeing things! That face, that *mask*—it's nothing but my imagination!

I take a shuddering breath, letting the cool cave air fill my lungs. It's... okay. I'm okay. Slowly, ever so slowly, I open my eyes once again; they meet Yulia's, with an unasked question on her lips.

"N-No," I force out. "...Please, don't worry about me. I'm fine now. It was just... a spell."

"Are you sure?"

"Yes. Thank you, Yulia. But, I'm fine now. Chin up, right?" I force my frozen face into a shaky smile, one she returns.

"That's the spirit. ...All the same, though, it'll be getting dark soon—let's return to the cavern. I'll finish showing you around the tunnels tomorrow."

The sun outside is already starting to set, by the time we return to the cavern, and the otherworldly blue light from this afternoon has already been replaced by the gentle orange glow of the setting sun, spilling in through the hole in the cavern ceiling. Yulia sees me settled in as best she can on the large flat rock that she's been using for a bed, then she lies herself down next to me.

With her by my side, I ask, "...Why did you want to know what Clarissa looks like?"

"Well..." Yulia gives a sheepish laugh. "I know it's a long shot, but you ended up here, right? Then..."

"Yulia... thank you."

She laughs, again. "You don't need to keep thanking me like that, you know. You'd do the same for me, wouldn't you?"

"Of course. As long as I don't have to swim."

We both giggle, at that.

"Um..." I search through my memories of my sister, clenching my fists against the sudden ache in my chest. It's strange—even though I'd know Clarissa immediately if I saw her, I can't find the words to describe her. "Well... Clarissa is, she's taller than I am. She has longer hair, too—just past the shoulder, the same black as mine. A-And her eyes! They're brown, just like mine. And, and... she's—she's very kind, with a smile like the sun, and..."

The moment I start to speak, the words start spilling from my mouth. At the same time, the more I speak, the worse the ache in my chest grows, until eventually—

"Clarissa...!" I break down, sobbing.

"Mary!? Are you all right?"

"N-No. I, I'm not," I choke out. Shaking my head, I swipe at the warmth overflowing from my eyes. "I'm not, b-but... I need this. Everything's going to be all right, isn't it? That's why—until then..."

Yulia simply holds me tight, and strokes my hair. Clarissa used to do the exact same thing. The moment I recognize—let myself recognize that, something inside me just breaks.

"Y-Yulia...! Yulia!"

"That's right, let it all out. Don't worry, I'm right here. Everything's going to be all right, I promise."

Lying on my back, I look up at the cavern ceiling, and the night sky beyond. It's a patch of midnight, without the light of a single star. The perfect mirror of our circumstances here, then. As if last night wasn't enough, here I am trapped on an island who knows where, with rescue nothing more than a distant dream.

If it wasn't for Yulia, reassuring me that 'everything is going to be all right', I'm sure I'd have gone insane by now. And so, in the dark, I call out to her. "Yulia."

"What is it, Mary?"

"...I just wanted to say, I'm glad you're here. Truly. If it wasn't for you..."

"You're making me blush, Mary." Yulia laughs, a little sheepishly. "...You know, it's horribly selfish of me to say so, but I'm glad I met you too. I mean, it's terrible, what happened to you. But..."

"Yes. At least we're not alone now, right? I..."

I'm just about to say something else, when—all of a sudden, an unearthly bellow echoes through the caves.

"What's going on!?" I sit up, clutching my makeshift blanket of rags tight as I peer into the darkness, in vain.

Beside me, Yulia just giggles. "It's all right, Mary, you can relax."

"B-But... that sound..."

"Don't worry. It's just the wind, I promise."

"The wind?"

"It happens every night, like clockwork, so it has to be." Yulia pauses, and gives me an apologetic pat on the head. "I'm sorry. I meant to warn you, but... I forgot."

I sigh in relief. "Yulia! Please don't forget about something like that! I had the fright of my life."

"I'm sorry, truly. ...I guess I've just gotten too used to it—I mean, I was scared at first, but now it's actually kind of relaxing, so..."

"Relaxing." Yulia can't be serious.

"It is! It sounds a little like church bells, doesn't it? The ones they ring every evening. I live... lived next to a church, and I swear it does."

...Now that she mentions it, I suppose it, charitably, might? At any rate, I let my breath out with a sigh. Regardless of what the noise is supposed to sound like—a bull bellow, to my ears—it can't be anything to be afraid of, not if Yulia so blasé about it. I lie back down on our rock bed, feeling all the tension drain out of me as I do.

"...Well, then... good night, Yulia."

"Good night, Mary. Sweet dreams."

* * *

I open my eyes to the darkness of midnight, as I sit up with a gasp, drenched with sweat. Slowly, I blink—once, twice—and confirm my surroundings.

I'm... in the cavern, on our rock bed. Beside me is Yulia, fast asleep, her gentle breathing breaking the monotony of the night and the thumping drum-beat of my heart pulsing in my ears. Shaking my head, I sigh. Just... just a dream.

I lie back down on our rock, closing my eyes once again. But, now that I'm awake I simply can't get back to sleep. I toss and turn on my makeshift rag blanket, trying to find... if not a more comfortable position, then at least one less uncomfortable. In vain, of course. Nonetheless, I'm so occupied I very nearly don't notice the light.

It's only when I hear that queer, bull's bellow noise from earlier, my eyes snapping open despite themselves at the sound, that I notice the eerie cobalt glow spilling into the cavern from the tunnel leading to the sea. And, at the same time, I realize: there's something *else* there by the tunnel, as well. A... a person? I don't know, and before I can find out it melts into the glow and disappears.

"I-Is someone there?"

There is, of course, no reply. Something, as much curiosity as fear, wells up inside me. I get down from the rock bed, doing my best not to disturb Yulia as I do. The stone floor sends needles of cold through the soles of my feet, and I bite back a yelp. Crossing the cavern, I enter the tunnel leading to the sea, where the light is coming from.

The noise grows louder with every cautious step I take. One, two, three—soon I'm swallowed up inside that sound, the hollow ringing of church bells filling me. And, enveloped as I am, I realize I can make out a voice hidden inside the bull's bellow—a woman's voice, singing a lullaby I know!

"Clarissa!"

I hasten my steps, the uncertainty of my footing forgotten. I'm a moth, drawn to a flame; the nearer I get to that light the more intensely it glows, and the further away everything else seems. The tunnel, the walls, the floor—everything starts to splinter around me, shattering into shards of a faraway dream. By the time I reach the tunnel exit, the only thing I know is that familiar, painfully familiar voice.

And then, I step out into the grotto where I woke up this afternoon. The night wind is bitterly cold, cutting at me like a knife. I don't, can't, pay it any mind. By the cave mouth, looking out to sea, is... *her*.

She's wearing nothing but a cotton camisole and bloomers, twins to mine. Her black hair, reaching just past her shoulders, dances in the wind. My breath turns to ice inside my lungs.

"C-Clarissa...? Is it really you?"

With a mind of its own, my body takes a step towards her. I can't believe it! I'd hoped, but I'd never dreamed I'd find...

Dreamed. I freeze. No, no. That's right—this has to be a dream. How else could she be here, as if by magic? No. Shaking my head, I start to take a step back, when...

She turns around, and the ice around my heart shatters into blessed warmth.

"Clarissa!"

I can't stop myself. It's really her! Launching myself into her arms, I wrap her in mine. She's cold as the grave, as cold as death frozen over. But, she's definitely flesh and bone, in my arms.

"I'm so glad...! I'm so glad you're all right! Thank God!"

I bury my face into her shoulder, sobbing. Oh, even though... even though I'd promised myself I wasn't going to cry! My tears simply refuse to stop.

Just then, though, the wind starts to pick up again, bringing me back to reality. I shiver, in the sudden chill. How much worse it must be for Clarissa, with her clothes drenched as they are. Releasing her from my embrace, I take her hand in mine.

"Come on, Clarissa, let's get inside. You must be freezing out here. There's not much, but we have water, and a bed, and..."

I tug at her arm. But, she doesn't budge.

"Clarissa...?"

I look up into her face, then, and—for the first time this night—she looks back at me. Her black hair, dripping with seawater. Her pale skin, corpse white. And, her eyes, two orbs of black mud.

Finally, I realize. This isn't a dream at all. It's a nightmare.

I open my mouth to scream. 'Clarissa' does the same—but, instead of words, it's a torrent of seawater that pours out. The brackish tide washes me away, staining my vision that same muddy black, and...

* * *

The gentle touch of a cool hand on my forehead calls me back from the black land of the unseeing. I open my eyes, to find myself looking into Yulia's.

"...Good morning, Mary." She gives me a small smile. "Bad dreams?"

"...Yulia?" My voice is hoarse, scratched raw. Sitting up, I look around me. I'm... on top of our 'bed', just like I was last night. The cavern is filled with gentle blue light, and I can see the clear morning sky through the hole in the cavern ceiling, feel the sun's warmth on my skin. Thank God—this is reality.

"I-I'm fine now." I shake my head. "Just a nightmare, that's all."

Yulia strokes my hair. "I guess it can't be helped, not after what you've been through. What's important is you're awake now. So, how about we get up?"

Getting down from our bed, I head over to the cavern pool and give my face a splash of cold water. The sudden chill against my skin causes me to yelp, but it also wakes my brain up—casting the mists of my dreams aside, in the bargain. Returning to our rock bed, I pick my clothes up from where I'd left them to dry last night. They're still a little damp, but worlds apart from yesterday's mess, and the moist cotton is only mildly unpleasant against my skin as I get dressed. By the time I'm finished, I can't remember even hints of my dream. What a fool I am, waking up so scared—am I a child of six all over again?

Already dressed, Yulia looks me over before cracking a grin. "There. You look more alive already."

"It was just a dream, after all." I give her a shy smile. "...I don't even remember what it was about."

"Well, that's how dreams are. More importantly, though, let's get going."

"Go?" I frown, lost. "Go where?"

"Breakfast, of course."

Like yesterday, Yulia leads me through the caves. Today, however, we don't go into that maze of tunnels beyond the cavern. Instead...

"Yulia, where are we going? This just leads back to the sea."

"Of course, silly." Yulia laughs. "Where did you think yesterday's fish came from?"

I feel my cheeks flush. She's right.

Yulia's smile turns apologetic. "Hey, don't get me wrong, Mary. I wasn't making fun of you. I just..."

"I know. I'm... just embarrassed, I suppose. I wasn't thinking."

"Geez, Mary. You've had a rough enough time so far—there's no need to be so hard on yourself. You should relax, and... oh, right." Cutting herself off, Yulia points out a tunnel branching off from the one we're in. It blends in almost perfectly with the surrounding tunnel walls, so well I'd completely overlooked it until now.

"Over here." Taking my hand, Yulia guides me down the narrow passage. The stone walls close in around us, and there's barely enough room to walk—or to breathe, it feels like—but it doesn't take long before we emerge once again into sunlight.

I gasp. Spreading out before my eyes is an expanse of sapphire, as the cave opens up and out into a lagoon. Rolling clouds of morning fog drift across the water's surface, past the rocky arms sheltering us from the sea, and seagulls wheel and soar high above, their cries joining the waves's gentle lullaby. It's beautiful.

Yulia makes her way over to the far end of the cave, just before where the floor sinks into the water, and picks up a... stick?—that was propped up against the wall. Resting it on her shoulder, she turns to me with a grin. "Mary, meet my partner. It's thanks to this I'm still alive."

I walk over to join her, taking a closer look at the stick. But, no matter how I look at it, that's all that I can see it as. I give up, and ask. "What is it?"

Yulia's grin turns sheepish. "A fishing spear. Or, well, a good impression of one."

"...You mean, you've been using that to fish?"

"Since I was seven, sure. I mean, it might be a little primitive, but it's real easy to use, and it's all I had on hand, so..."

"You mean you caught all those fish yesterday with this? That's amazing! I couldn't do something like that in a hundred years."

"It's nothing special, really!" Yulia's tanned cheeks burn red. "Anyone could do this with a little practice. I'll teach you—once we get you something to eat, of course. Just wait here, I'll be right back with breakfast."

Producing the knife from yesterday out of one of her pockets, Yulia retrieves a strip of cloth from another and lashes the knife to her arm. Slipping out of her clothes, she folds them neatly and lays them down on the cave floor. Then, she runs—and dives into the water with a splash!

Yulia's movements are poetry, as she cuts through the water. Reaching the far off center of the lagoon, she turns and gives me a wave. "Just wait right there!" She calls out; then, she's gone, disappeared under the water with barely a ripple.

* * *

I sigh, as I wait for Yulia to return from the lagoon with breakfast. I've never felt quite as useless as I do now. I knew I should have learnt how to swim, or at least try to. What good does being able to waltz do me now? All the same, Yulia told me to wait, so here I am, waiting.

It can't have been a minute since Yulia started fishing, and already it feels like an eternity to useless me. Worse still, and perhaps from all I've been through since the *Bastion*, but the moments-ago warm and welcoming morning sun's now harsh light starts causing pain to arc between my temples.

As I squeeze my eyes shut against the migraine growing beneath my skull, through the pain I hear a sound, one no longer muffled by that world shaking drone, but clear as day—that voice.

Nausea rises up inside me; the scent of the sea, rotted fish and bitter salt, fills my mouth, and black spots dance across my vision. I close my eyes, tight, and shake my head as hard as I can, to no avail. Mud starts to ooze, from the insides of my eyes—its black corruption *seeps* into me, staining everything that horrible oily black, and I know nothing else.

The next time I open my eyes, I'm in the grotto where I woke up yesterday, looking down into the water. From beneath the waves, *it* looks back.

My blood freezes in my veins, every nerve in my body writhing. That face, reflected in the water—it's an exact mirror of mine. But where my eyes should be are... two black orbs of mud.

"No."

Sour bile rises in my throat. This... this can't be happening. I'm seeing things, or having a dream, or...

"M-M-Mary..."

"No!"

"Mary... come join me, M-Mary. Join us. W-We're waiting for you."

"No... no, no, no!"

"Come home, Mary. We... C-Clarissa is waiting for you... I-I-I... am waiting for you..."

An icicle of pain stabs through my heart, that suddenly familiar voice worming its way into my mind. Despite myself, tears come to my eyes.

"M-Mother...? Mother, is that—!?"

"Mary!"

Sea rotted hands burst from the water, wrapping themselves around my neck.

"Come home, Mary! Come home!"

I try to scream, I try to struggle. But, as ragged fingernails tear at my throat and fingers strong as steel tighten around my neck, all I can manage is a strangled gasp. Slowly, slowly, I'm pulled closer to the water's surface.

If I let myself be pulled under, I'm dead. But, even so, I can't do a thing to resist. Closer and closer the hands pull me, to the water's surface—and that *thing*. My lungs burn, darkness devours my vision, and I know: this is the end for me. I'll die here, drowned by a monster that wears my face. Yulia...

"No!"

I scream, wringing every last shred of strength I have out of myself, tearing at the hands around my neck. And, even as the 'me' beneath the waves widens her eyes in shock, I win free and throw myself backwards, away from the cave mouth, the sea.

The *thing* screams, a banshee's howl. Leaping from the waves, it hurls itself at me. But, even as its terrible claws reach for my throat, the monster simply... dissolves, into sea spray.

I'm left, alone—alive—in the grotto, the only sound besides the waves my shuddering breaths. My neck burns, the pain giving the lie to what happened being just a dream. Faced with that pain, I...

"No... no... I don't want this. I don't..."

Moaning, I curl up and hug myself tight. My head hurts, aching like an overripe, rotted grape. There's something inside me, inside my skull pushing and pulling and squeezing, and it hurts so much I want to just vomit and vomit and vomit until there's nothing left inside.

I'm so, so tired. And so, with the waves lulling me to sleep, I—

"Mary! Stop! Don't do it!"

"No!"

I squeeze my eyes shut against the voice calling my name. No! Leave me alone! I, I—!

"Mary!" Wet feet slap against the cavern floor. She calls my name once more, and... "Mary. Mary, it's me." Warmth envelops me, her warm hands holding me back from the muddy dark.

"Y-Yulia...?"

"Yes. Yes, it's me. Don't worry, I'm here now. It's... everything's going to be all right."

Something inside me shatters. Everything, all of me, spills away, and I simply... sink, into that dark sea of unconsciousness.

* * *

I awaken from dreams of dark waters and darker mud to find myself in our cavern, on our rock bed. For a moment I just lie there, staring up at the cavern ceiling, and the afternoon sky beyond.

It... hurts. My whole body aches, and my throat burns with a dull fire. Running my fingers over my neck, I discover several small crescent wounds, only recently scabbed over. Did I... cut myself on something? I-I don't remember, and that *emptiness* in my memory causes terror to well up inside me.

Clenching my hands tight against the panic rising up inside me, feeling the sensation of my nails—nails?—digging into my palm, I force myself to relax. Calm down, Mary, you need to calm down. Everything comes after that.

Slowly, breath by deep breath, the tightness in my chest loosens, and the pain coursing through my body eases. I try to sit up, now that it doesn't feel like I'd snap myself in two with the effort, and...

"Mary!" From the cavern pool, Yulia comes running. Resting her hands on my shoulders, she pushes me, gently but firmly, back down onto our 'bed'. "It's still too early for you to be getting up. You need your rest, after... after what happened."

"Happened...?" Again, that sensation of loss, of forgetting something terribly important. I, I...

At my question, Yulia's eyes widen. "You don't remember? But, you were going to—your neck..."

The world tilts, a wave of nausea rising up inside me. Something... *something* happened, I'm sure. But... "Please, Yulia, tell me. Did something happen to me?"

"I..." For the longest time, Yulia doesn't meet my gaze. With her expression clouded, she simply stares at the wounds on my neck. Finally, though, she gives me a shaky smile. "No... no, nothing happened. You were just... you fainted, while I was fishing for breakfast."

"But... then, the wounds on my neck...?"

Yulia blinks, before shaking her head. "I... don't know. You must have fallen on a rock, or maybe scraped yourself against... something. I'm sorry, Mary. I didn't notice something had happened to you until I surfaced, so..."

"Oh." So Yulia doesn't know what happened either. But, what she said makes sense. Yes, that's right. I must have fainted, and fallen poorly on... something sharp. That has to be it.

At any rate, "I'm sorry, Yulia. I must have made you worry."

Yulia sighs, her expression melting into a gentle smile. "You did! ...Please, Mary. If you feel unwell, or... or strange, or anything like that, let me know. Promise me."

I nod, slowly, and squeeze my eyes shut against the sudden warmth threatening to overflow from them. "I promise, Yulia."

A pat, on my head. "Thank you, Mary. Don't worry.

144

Everything's going to be all right. ...And, more importantly, now that you're awake let's get you something to eat. I'll be right back."

The end of dinner finds me lying on our rock bed, looking up at the fast darkening sky through the hole in the cavern ceiling. Returning from dumping our meal's refuse in the sea, Yulia lies down beside me. For what feels like an eternity the two of us just lie there, the only sound in the cavern our breathing.

"Yulia." Eventually, though, I'm the one who breaks the silence.

"Mary? What is it?" Rolling over to put us face to face, Yulia asks.

I pause. Maybe... maybe it would be better to not say anything, to brush it off as nothing. But, somehow, something inside me wouldn't let me. Especially, not with my memories—rather, my lack of them—of yesterday.

"Do you... do you really think everything's going to be all right?"

"Of course! I mean, someone's bound to come searching for me, or the ship you were on, and..."

145

"Yulia." I call her name, and she trails off. Then, reaching over, she takes my hand in hers.

"...I know what you're trying to say, Mary. Even if they do notice, what are the odds they'll know it's this island, out of all the others? And, even if they do eventually get here..." Yulia shakes her head. "I don't know, Mary. Honestly. But, that goes both ways, doesn't it?"

"Both ways?"

"Help... help might never come. On the other hand, help might come tomorrow. Who's to say?"

"That's..."

"We don't know, do we? Only God does. So... why don't we believe?"

"That's..." Ridiculous, I start to say. But, something stops me. Rather, I stop me. Why don't we believe? If we can't help anything either way, why not? And so, instead, I nod. "...You're right, Yulia."

"Of course I am! After all..."

We share a grin, and fill the cavern with laughter. "Everything's going to be all right."

As the last of the sun's orange madder fades from the sky,

a thought suddenly strikes me. For a while now there's been something about how Yulia's presence relaxed me that I couldn't understand. At last, though, I get it. "Do you have any siblings, Yulia? You mentioned your parents before, but..."

Yulia nods, next to me in the dark. "Yup. Well, technically they're just cousins, but they're like brothers and sisters to me. I'm the oldest, can you believe that?"

"No wonder. I was just thinking, you seem like such an older sister." I giggle.

"I certainly feel that way, dealing with them." Yulia chuckles. Then, in a more sombre tone. "What about you, Mary? You said you were on your way to see relatives, but...?"

I nod. "Yes, my mother's. Father was... busy, with work, so he didn't join us, but it was supposed to be a family trip."

"Then, your mother... No, never mind."

"It's all right. Mother... she wasn't on the *Bastion* with us."

It's as if I'm looking at the two of us from someplace far-off. Even though I'd burst into tears just thinking about it, a few months ago, right now all I feel is a dull, hollow ache inside my chest. It's as if that terrible wound in my heart has finally scabbed over, like the ones on my neck. And so, although it's still terribly unsteady, I'm at least able to give Yulia a small smile as I answer.

"Mother... died half a year ago, in a rowing accident."

"Oh." Yulia bites her lip, her expression clouding. "Mary, I'm sorry."

"No, it's fine. I'm sure she wouldn't want me stuck thinking about her, not at a time like this."

"Still. ...If I lost my mother, if I could never see her again..." Yulia trails off, her voice choked.

I roll over, and take her into my arms. Just like she did for me, I stroke her hair, and whisper to her: "Don't worry, Yulia. Everything is going to be all right, isn't it? You'll see her again. I promise."

"...You too, Mary." Yulia returns my embrace with interest, holding me so tight it feels like I might break. "You're going to see your family again. And, until then, I'll protect you—I swear."

That night, I didn't dream. Not of black mud, or of the sea. Just, nestled within Yulia's arms, I slept.

* * *

Days passed, weeks, a month—how long it's been since that night, I don't know. Just, little by little, I got used to life on our island prison. We—Yulia and I—settled into a routine, of sorts.

First, a breakfast of fresh fish, to start the day. After tidying up we'd go to the lagoon, where Yulia would teach me how to swim and fish. "Just in case."

Around noon we'd break for lunch, eating the fish I—or more likely, Yulia—had caught. After that, we'd rest for a while. Sometimes, by swimming and floating in the lagoon; other times, by exploring the maze of tunnels that ran through the island. Mostly, though, we'd just talk. About our families, or what we'd do once we got home, the first non-fish meal we'd eat. My skin grew darker by the day, and it wasn't long before I had a tan matching Yulia's.

Around sunset, we'd have dinner. As we ate, we'd look out across the sea, at the distant horizon. I don't know what Yulia thought, looking at the sun sinking into the sea; as for me, though, my thoughts returned time and time again to Father. What would he be doing now, I wonder? Worrying about Clarissa and I? ...Or, would he be so occupied with his practice that we'd be just another note at the bottom of his schedule, something else he'd be too busy to bother with?

With sunset came bedtime. Without any light of our own there was hardly anything else we could do, but sleep. I never managed to before Yulia. With her presence next to me a lullaby rocking me to sleep, I'd just look up at that patch of the night in the cavern ceiling and think.

Eventually, of course, sleep would come, stealing me away into blissful oblivion—and far less blissful dreams. I had no more nightmares, not since that night. But all the same, my dreams were filled with black mud, and blacker, formless things still. Even so, I was glad for those dreams. They were a testament, of sorts, to another day survived.

That day too, started like any other.

I awake to sunrise, and the warm light of the morning sun. Rubbing the sleep from my eyes, I've just gotten dressed when Yulia returns to our cavern with the day's breakfast—a monster of a fish, one nearly as long as my shoulders are wide. Seeing me already up, she gives me a cheery smile.

"Good morning, Mary. Wait just a minute, okay? I'll have breakfast ready in a second." Setting the fish down on the cave floor, Yulia draws her fishing knife from its cloth sheath and gets to work. There isn't an ounce of waste to her movements, as she carves it up. She's even humming, as she works—a cheerful tune, but not one cheerful enough to disguise the bags under her eyes.

All the same, I know what she'll say if I bring them up, so instead I just give her a small smile. "You're in a good mood today."

"Of course! I never thought I'd catch anything this big in shallow waters, and... oh, here we go." Cutting a fillet off the fish, Yulia hands it to me with a grin. "Here, Mary, your share."

"Thank you, Yulia." Taking the fish in my hands, I sit quietly and wait. Soon, Yulia's done preparing hers, too, and we begin the day's breakfast.

Chasing the last of her meal down with a gulp of water, Yulia gives a playful burp.

I sigh. "You're being unrefined again, Yulia." All the same, I can't help but smile.

Leaning back, she yawns. "You're too uptight, Mary. It's not like there's anyone to hear, is there?"

"Maybe, but what are you going to do when we get back home?"

"I guess you're right." Stifling another yawn, she gives me a sheepish grin.

"...Did you wake up early again?" Frowning, I lean over to look up into her face. Not that I need to, when I know what I'll find. The bags under Yulia's eyes are terrible.

But, she just laughs. "Give me a break, Mary, I can't help it. Just lying down all the time would drive me insane."

"Still. ...Why don't you get some rest? I'll handle today's lunch."

Yulia's easy smile disappears, as does any trace of fatigue. "No way. What if you had an accident? It's too early for you to be swimming alone."

"Now who's the uptight one? I'll be fine."

"Like that time with the puffer fish?"

"I'll check with you before I eat anything, I promise. You need your sleep."

"If you got a cramp..."

"You swim by yourself all the time."

"I'm different. ...Please, Mary. What if you fainted out there?"

Yulia and I stare at each other, not an ounce of give in either of our gazes. But, I know there's no winning against her when she digs her heels in like this, so... "Okay. I understand, Yulia. But, promise me you'll get some rest."

She cracks a bitter smile. "I guess there's no helping it. I'll just lie down for a bit, then. You'll wake me when it's time to fish for lunch?"

I put my hands on my hips. "You just worry about napping, okay?"

Yulia sighs. "Fine, fine. I get it already, Mary. ...Night."

Yulia heads for our bed, lying down amidst our rag blankets. I watch her out of the corner of my eye, as I gather the fish bones and scaly skins to throw away in the sea. Even before I leave the cavern, she's already fast asleep.

I laugh, softly. "Even though you're already this tired... You're too stubborn for your own good, Yulia."

I didn't notice at first, of course. Not how she woke up early every morning to fish, just so I'd have something ready to eat; nor how she made it a point to stay by my side, in case I fainted again. I was just too busy thinking about myself, about Clarissa, that I didn't notice just how much Yulia thought of me.

The moment I did notice, I was so embarrassed, so ashamed, that I wanted to just crawl into a hole and disappear. There I was, unable to do a single thing, living off someone's kindness all over again. Useless, just like six months ago.

When I return to the cavern from dumping our garbage into the sea, it's already started. Clutching her rag blanket tight, Yulia twists and turns atop our rock bed, her face contorted with pain.

"No, no... Ma, Pa, I... I..." She moans, tears flowing down her cheeks.

I always sleep after Yulia, so I know. Lately, she's been like this every night. In a way, it's only logical. While she's been protecting me, from my dreams and worse, who's been protecting her?

I smooth Yulia's hair, and give her a kiss on the cheek. It might have been my imagination, but she relaxes ever so slightly, at that. I smile. "Don't worry, Yulia. Just like how you protect me, I'll protect you. I promise."

That's right. This time, it's my turn to do something for her. Taking the fishing knife from where Yulia left it on the cave floor, and its cloth sheath, I head for the lagoon.

I squint my eyes against the sudden light, as I emerge from the tunnels into the cave that leads to the lagoon. Slipping out of my tattered camisole and bloomers, I lash the fishing knife to my arm the way I've seen Yulia do a thousand times, then I pick up our fishing spear and step into the lagoon.

It's a beautiful day, with the sun high in the sky and not a cloud in sight. The water's surface glimmers under the noon sun, rippling around my ankles as I ease my way into the water. Pushing off from the rock shelf, where the cave sinks into the bay, I go further and further into the lagoon until finally there's nothing to stand on.

Taking a deep breath, I tighten my grip on the fishing spear and squeeze my eyes shut; then, I dive. As always, the sensation of water on my face tells me its time to ease my eyes open—I do, and what greets me is a riot of coral color, with an accompanying phantasmagoria of fish.

From the rainbow labyrinth of corals around me, to the gentle luminescence coming from the undersea tunnels that honeycomb the base of the island, the lagoon is as beautiful as always.

So much so, in fact, it takes my brain a moment to process the body floating by the lagoon 'mouth'.

The air in my lungs freezes, reality a hammer to the glass wonder around me.

'It' was floating by the reef that cut the lagoon off from the sea proper, its leg caught on a spur of coral. Bobbing in the crystal clear water, and clothed in a waterlogged brown suit, it resembled nothing so much as driftwood. Save, that is, for the tortured rictus upon its face. As I swim closer for a better look, my eyes meet its unseeing orbs, and tendrils of ice coil around my heart.

I know that face, this man.

He... his name was Mister Worthington, and he was a fellow passenger on the *Bastion*. He was a kindly old man, two cabins down from mine and Clarissa's, and he was visiting family, in the New World. He had a grand-daughter, he said, just about my age.

Tears run down my cheeks unbidden. I... I'd known people must have died, with what happened to the *Bastion*. But, I knew him.

It isn't right! Why did he have to die like this, cast about by the sea's waves like so much garbage? That there isn't anyone else to care, that there isn't anything for a proper grave, is just too cruel. But, most of all—after seeing him like this, what am I supposed to think about Clarissa?

I can't just leave him here, floating like this. How could I? And so, reaching out, I make to drag his body back to the caves. That was when it happened.

Mister Worthington twitches, a herky-jerky dead man's dance. His unseeing eyes rolled, in their sockets, to follow mine. They cloud, and fill with black mud—to bursting, his ruptured eyeballs spilling obscene tears. Mister Worthington—*it*—seized and thrashed, dead-man's teeth flashing, and I scream as they bury themselves in my outstretched hand.

I didn't mean to, I swear. I didn't! But, even before I can process what happened my body moves on its own, sending the fishing spear forward in a wild stab—one that plunges right into Mister Worthington's pallid throat.

The sick shock of wood burying itself in meat, then bone, reverberates through my arm; *its* jaws spring open in a wordless scream, one I give voice to even as I pull my hand free.

Thick black oil pours from his throat, spreading through the water like macabre ink. And even despite the that terrible wound, Mister Worthington's gray and rotting fingers continue to claw at me, grasping at my still bleeding hand. I push him away with a cry—and then, I dive, away.

I swim faster than I'd ever thought I could, as if I was possessed, practically flying through the undersea tunnels where I sought refuge. A branch, here; there, a side-passage; terror robs me of everything, everything but the need to get away.

By the time I realize my mistake, it's too late. I return to myself in a narrow, cobalt-glowing tunnel, its walls of smooth turquoise stone closing in around me.

There's barely enough room to go forward, and none to turn back, with no end to the tunnel in sight—and precious little sight to begin with, despite the glowing luminescence of the walls.

The only thing I can do is keep moving forward—I don't have enough air left in my lungs to try and turn around. With that realization, every nerve in my body begins to squirm, like a million tiny worms beneath my skin. The strength my frantic flight gave me fades, to be replaced with a leaden fear. Already, black spots are starting to dance at the edge of my vision, and my lungs burn.

I'm going to die here. Like Mister Worthington, like... Clarissa.

What would Yulia think? She'd wake to find me gone, the fate I'd escaped so long ago finally caught up with me. No! I can't—won't—do that to her! My determination crystallizes into strength. I push myself forward, hard as I can, and...

Far ahead, impossibly far, an alien blue light shines through the tunnel to reveal its end. I plunge forward, towards that blue salvation. And then, like a lost soul through the gates of heaven, I pull myself up into the light, and emerge into blessed air.

* * *

Coughing, I pull myself up through a hole in an unfamiliar cave's floor to emerge into a place I've never seen before. Filling my lungs with sweet air, I take a look around.

The cave I'm in is about the size of the cavern I share with Yulia; it has walls of cloudy turquoise stone, and a large—about as wide across as I am tall—marble orb embedded in its center.

The orb glowed with an otherworldly light, one that filled the room and, as if acknowledging my gaze, began to pulse. I take a step towards it, a moth to the flame. One step, two steps, three—the orb pulls me to it, drawing me closer and closer despite myself. With every step I take, the farther away everything else gets. Soon I'm standing right in front of the orb, and an eternity from anything else.

As flawless and smooth the marble orb looked from far away, this close I can make out a labyrinthine web of carvings on its surface. Here, a fish; there, a school of sharks. Octopi, lobsters and crabs, whales; and, on the very apex of the dome—a man, yet not a man. Fins sprouted from its misshapen limbs, and there were gills carved into its neck. Most inhuman of all, though, was its face: a smooth mask of flesh, adorned with a single unblinking onyx eye.

Thump. The moment I look into that *eye*, my whole body tenses.

"What... what is this?"

My voice echoes in the chamber, as heavy and ponderous as the ringing of church-bells. I reach out, my hand dancing on an unseen puppeteer's strings, drawn to that orb, that eye.

The moment my fingers make contact with the orb's marble surface, all light in the cave dies. And, from the darkness...

"M-Mary..."

I hear her voice again, stuttering and weak, but soft and warm and gentle—the voice of family.

"Mother? Mother, is that you?"

From behind me, footsteps—wet feet, against stone. They come to a stop behind me.

"Mary... I missed you, M-Mary. W-W-Welcome... home."

A wet, grave-cold hand caresses my shoulder, and I know.

"...No. You're not Mother."

It might only be a little, but I remember enough. A night, a dream, six months ago; my first night on this island, the first time I saw 'it'. I narrow my eyes at the hateful thing before me.

"You're not Mother. She's dead. She... she isn't coming back."

The hand atop my shoulder disappears, melting into the darkness, as does the voice. In its place...

"M-Mary. Don't... worry, Mary. W-W-We'll be safe in here. The *Bastion* is a fine... s-ship, and the c-captain is a good... man."

"Stop it!"

I scream, pitting my voice against its—*her*—whispering siren song.

"How dare you! How dare you use her voice like that! You're not Clarissa!"

"I... a-am, Mary. Don't you r-r-recognize... me?"

"Shut up!"

I tear the fishing knife from its sheath, and brandish it high. Warmth, bitter warmth, flows down my cheeks.

It growls.

"Mary, M-Mary... You are... mine. My daughter, m-my sister... Mine!"

Sea-rotted hands close around my throat, ragged nails digging deep into my flesh. I scream.

"Mary... Come and join us, Mary. Come back home. Close your eyes, Mary. Close your eyes, and y-y-you can see us again."

...This is just, too cruel. Even though, even though I know it's lying, I, I—

"No!"

I bring the knife down, through my own hand, into the center of the orb's eye.

Light flares, a newborn sun igniting beneath my fingers. Thunder booms and lightning cracks, as cracks spiderweb across the orb's surface. For a single, frozen moment, I stare into a void deeper than the sea itself—the next, and a woman screams as the orb implodes in a flash of oily black light.

Water roars, as the sea pours into the cave. I just close my eyes, and let myself disappear.

"Mary! Mary, you're all right! Thank God! I looked everywhere for you!"

"Yu...lia...?"

"Mary...?"

"...Sister. S-S-Sister. ...Sister? Are... you crying? Does it... h-hurt?"

"...No. I'm... I'm fine. Come on, Mary, let's get you dried off and dressed."

"...Okay."

"Don't worry, Mary. Everything's... everything's going to be all right, I promise."

fin

Commentary/Cast

Blue First Kiss

A story about jealousy and immaturity. I wanted to write a story contrasting platonic love with romantic love, and explore the difference between a 'best friend' and a 'girlfriend' for girls. The only story here where the girls have image songs. Tsukasa-chan's is 'Waikyou: Shen Shou Jin' by Iguchi Yuka, while Seiko's is the 'Romeo and Cinderella' cover(?) by Otouto no Ane. Um. Someday I want to write a story where Seiko gets to find her own happiness.

- Mitsuki Aoi

密月　葵

An ordinary girl with a not-so-ordinary last name. She's quite certain she's a lesbian, considering she's in love with another girl, but she isn't sure what she's supposed to do as one, exactly. A bit of a show-off in front of people she likes, but essentially 'normal', otherwise. Just, a little oblivious, when it comes to other people's feelings. She has quite a complex about her above-average height. A member of the student council, although she mostly just does the busy work.

- Hiramoto Tsukasa

平本　つかさ

None other than the girl Aoi's in love with. She first met Aoi through the student council, of which she's a much relied-upon member. Has a reputation for being smart, hard-working and kind, but she just might have a bit of a selfish side? Loves astronomy, astrology, and anything to do with the stars. Doesn't think small lies are a bad thing, necessarily. An only child, showered with love by her parents.

- Yagami Seiko

八神　清子

Aoi's best friend. Her family's from Kansai, but they moved to Aoi's town when she was still a baby—but, somehow, she still manages to have a Kansai accent. She's known Aoi since kindergarten, and loved her since middle school. A closeted otaku, she's currently working as a manga artist under a pen-name. Lives on her own, her parents having moved back to the west when she entered high school.

nostalgia fragrance

A story about the memories a familiar smell can bring, and—from halfway through, without my knowing—lying. Um. This is probably the story that changed the most from my initial 'image' to 'reality'. I like to think that one day, Ann is going to wake up married to Kuroe with no idea why, but not being that bothered by it.

- Ann

アン

A girl who tells the 'truth' as easily as she breathes. She's a 'half', her father having been a foreigner, but from where nobody but Ann knows. She's twenty-one, if you believe her, and surprisingly prone to anemia—karma, perhaps? A sworn cynic, but because it suits her, or... During Ann's first year in university her mother died, and since then Ann's dropped out and taken to living off part-time jobs.

- Kuroe

くろえ

Ann's co-worker. She's eighteen, a fresh university student, and just might have a history with Ann? She's been living on her own since starting university, and is your

166

classic over-achiever, somehow managing to find time from studying to work part-time as a hobby. Why, is a question best left unsaid. Her dream was to become an actress, but lately she's more than willing to settle for owning a small store and hiring a certain special someone to work there.

Infirmary Heart

A story about growing up and moving on, and the difference between an adult and a child, maybe. I originally just wanted to write a story set in the school infirmary, but somehow it ended up being an age-gap romance. I blame Ami-sensei.

- Kazumiya Izumi

一宮　泉

A high schooler in her final year, with just the slightest habit of playing sick. She looks fragile, but she's surprisingly stubborn when she wants to be. Comes from a family of traditional craftsmen, from a prefecture famous for its traditional art. She loves both, and has always dreamed of combining them when she takes over the family business—over her family's objections, who want her to study something with more of a 'future'. For some reason, she loves the short story 'The Gift of the Magi'.

- Yoshida Ami

吉田　亜美

Izumi's school nurse. Calm and collected, with a maturity that belies her relatively young age. She's an alumnus of the school, and thus an 'older sister' to the students under her care in more ways than one. Surprisingly childish in private, though, and ever so slightly addicted to caffeine. Short-sighted, she prefers wearing glasses to contacts, because she thinks the latter make her look too young.

In the Season of Falling Leaves

A story I always wanted to write, but ended up struggling with the most. Probably the story that affected me the most. I think, being in such a dark place, what's hardest isn't choosing to die, but choosing to live anyway. Really, I hope Yuri and Shizuho find happiness together.

- Kamoda Yuri

鴨田　ユリ

A girl stricken with a rare and degenerative disease. Already melancholic to start with, she's become an utter nihilist who can't find any meaning in continuing to live. The kind who lashes out when she's hurt, a classic hedgehog who can't help but push away the people she most wants to be with her. She's always had a crush on a certain friend of hers but could never find the courage to admit it, until things changed and it was too late to.

- Shizuho

靜恵

Yuri's best friend, and the only one who stayed by Yuri's side through the other girl's lashing out. In place of Yuri's family, Shizuho juggles university with taking care of her friend. Has a bad habit of procrastination, of putting the hard choices off for 'tomorrow'. But, when faced with the possibility of her world ending today...

The Lagoon of Eyes

A story about fighting against the great and terrible unknown, while sure you have no hope of winning. In that respect, it's a little like 'Falling Leaves', I think. My first horror story, but even now I'm not sure if it's scary enough to be horror. The setting is in an alternate, ever so slightly more eldritch world than ours. But, when, I have no idea. When did wooden passenger ships disappear, anyway? Well, that's probably another mystery of the island. If I write another story in this world one day, I'd really like to make it both more squamous and rugose.

- Mary Arkham

The second daughter of the Arkham family. Her father is from Albion high society, a patron of archeology, and runs both a practice and sanitarium; her mother fled from the turn of the century strife in New Ithaca, carrying a past she never shared with even her husband. Mary has always had a dislike of water, owing to persistent night-terrors of the sea. By the time she was born her parents were all but estranged, and so she has a complicated, but very close relationship with her older sister Clarissa.

- Yulia LeRoux

A young girl of Aquitaine blood, she lived with her parents and extended family in one of Albion's New World colonies. Fiercely protective of anyone she cares about, a learned instinct from long years of being the 'older sister' in a baker's dozen of children spread over three families. A quiet, but determined optimist always forcing herself to look for the best in every situation. But, is that positivity a blessing, or a curse?

Afterword

Hi, I'm Yuuki Haru. First of all, thanks for reading my book! If you liked it, or even if you didn't, why not take the time to leave a review at your favourite retailer? I'd really appreciate it.

Now, I'd like to talk a little about this collection. This book, 'spring: mutsuki', is a collection of short stories originally published on my website 'Kogepen-ya', from May 17th 2014 to May 16th, 2015. These are the first stories I've made public, and I can't say how amazing it feels to know I've produced an entire year's worth of them, compiled them into an actual book. So, again, thank you, reader. None of this would be possible without you.

Finally, this book, 'spring: mutsuki', might be at an end, but that doesn't mean there aren't any more stories to read. Why not check out my website, once again 'Kogepen-ya', where I publish both standalone and short story serials every other week?

Until we meet again,
Haru

www.ingramcontent.com/pod-product-compliance
Lightning Source LLC
Chambersburg PA
CBHW021046130626
46552CB00005B/2032